HAWKING'S HIGHWAY

D. E. Bench

HAWKING'S HIGHWAY

D. E. Bench

Salt Lake City
2021

Hawking's Highway

ISBN: 978-1-304-12694-8

First Printing: July 2021
Bench-Press Publishing
Salt Lake City, Utah

Dedicated to the memory of Stephen W. Hawking—

His lifelong search for knowledge and understanding provided

many answers—and more importantly, many more questions—

about our place in the cosmos.

And to my wife, Liesl—my heart's singularity,

whose perfect gravitational pull both keeps me grounded—

and allows me to soar.

"We are just an advanced breed of monkeys on a minor planet of a very average star. But we can understand the Universe. That makes us something very special." —Stephen Hawking

Chapter 1

From: *The Salt Lake Tribune* - April 5, 2023

Geologists Seek to End Debate Over Canyonlands Crater Origins

by Bryan Murphy:

The recent discovery of shocked quartz formations has geologists taking a new look at the Upheaval Dome structure in the desert of southeastern Utah. The crater's origins have long been a source of debate among scientists as to whether the formation resulted from a collapsed salt dome or an actual impact event. Formed in the late Cretaceous Period, the crater and nearby landscape have been subjected to significant weathering and erosion for 65–100 million years. These forces have removed much of the surrounding rock and soil, hampering efforts to fully understand the history of the site. This discovery has generated renewed interest in the area because shocked quartz formations are more often associated with meteor and asteroid impacts. Under the guidance of Geology Chair Thaddeus Sterling, Ph.D., a geoscientist team from the University of Utah has received special permission from the National Parks Service to excavate the crater for meteorite fragments to support this hypothesis.

The article includes Sterling's official faculty headshot, a smiling African American in his early sixties, meticulously dressed in a dark three-piece suit.

***

The wind sent small eddies of dust and fine sand across the arid desert floor. Richard Hayes shaded his eyes and glanced up to see the sun perched just above the jagged tip of gray-green rock. The formation protruded part-way from the crater's center like the fossilized navel of some giant prehistoric creature.

Red cliffs towered above him on three sides with tons of rock and sand deposited at their bases. Millions of years of relentless wind and water had washed away the crater wall to the west, replacing it with a narrow canyon. Now, this part of the desert was as dry as the surface of Mars. The occasional rain only washed away additional soil in a series of flash floods. They needed to finish the dig before Arizona's late summer monsoon rains would make working in the crater too dangerous and unpredictable.

Richard squatted in a freshly dug depression roughly five feet across and four feet deep. He had to be careful not to dig too deeply without widening the hole first. Doctor Sterling had cautioned Richard and the other grad students against taking unnecessary risks.

Doctor Sterling stood about twenty feet away, leaning in to discuss something with Susie. Her hole wasn't as deep; she was standing, and Richard could see her from the waist up. The other student, Declan, was digging just out of sight behind a large mound of earth. Eventually, Richard turned his attention back to his work.

Just a few more inches now, he thought, setting aside the bulkier hand-shovel in favor of the more delicate trowel. Richard began carefully scooping sand and rocks into the orange Home Depot bucket to his left. The tool struck something solid, and he could see a gray edge protruding from the red earth around it. The red sand spilled away, almost as if the object was pushing itself from the soil.

Richard reached into his tool pack, removed a stiff-bristled brush, and exposed a smooth, unblemished pentagonal surface with just a few quick strokes.

He initially thought it was a crystalline structure, as it resembled some pyrite examples he had seen—but pyrite crystals are cubic. This strange object was not a natural shape; its surface was too smooth, its dimensions too exact. A slight concavity sat in the center of its face, about a half-inch across. Whatever it was, it looked too clean to have been buried in the desert sand.

He called out to the others as he clambered to his feet.

"Doctor Sterling, I've found something. I think you need to see this."

***

Thaddeus Sterling stood dumbfounded among the three grad students, looking into Richard's freshly dug hole. For several days, the small team had excavated the site for what they assumed would be remnants of a nickel-iron meteorite. They had split up, with each student working at a different location identified by ground-penetrating radar. Doctor Sterling supervised and aided them when necessary. Neither Declan nor Susie had turned up anything significant, though, and Sterling had begun to rethink their process.

The object Richard had unearthed looked human-made, yet they'd found it buried several feet beneath packed earth and rock. Sterling pulled out a tape measure and began comparing each surface. Something about being this close to the object made his skin crawl.

"Someone, please write this down." His voice was quiet, almost a whisper. "Object appears to be a perfect dodecahedron, with sharp edges and a smooth, matte finish. The sides of each facet measure...thirty-one centimeters exactly. Each face bears an identical depression in its center—one point two-five centimeters across and half a centimeter deep."

He scooped up a handful of dust and sprinkled a light layer across the object. The tiny grains repeatedly bounced before finally settling lightly on the surface; however, no sand fell into the depression but instead seemed to disperse around it. He blew across it from side to side as one would extinguish birthday candles. The exterior was spotless; the red dust left no residue.

"The outer surface is an unknown material but appears metallic—perhaps an alloy. The artifact is uniformly gray in color. It repels dust and emanates a mild magnetic field," he continued. "The object has ..." He trailed off and stood transfixed, a look of pure concentration on his face.

Yang Shu—who went by Susie—watched him, concerned, her tablet and stylus still in hand.

"Doctor Sterling?" Her voice snapped him back from wherever he had gone. She glanced nervously at the others before continuing. "What do you think it is?"

"I have no idea," he said. "I'm sure I've never seen anything like this."

"Maybe it's a piece of a fallen satellite?" Richard chimed in.

"Satellites are made of lightweight materials," Declan said. "This t'ing's as dense as you are." His Irish brogue rolled off his tongue when he spoke.

Richard rolled his eyes at the larger man. For almost a week, Sterling had noted Richard's growing irritation with the Irish student, and for his part, Declan appeared to be purposely pushing Richard's buttons just to get a rise out of him. Richard seemed about to respond to Declan's comment, but Sterling sensed the beginnings of another heated exchange between the two and cut him off.

"I think we could all use a break."

***

Cell and internet coverage at the dig site was almost nonexistent, so periodic trips into the small desert town of Moab were essential for email and phone calls. It was a comfortable evening—the real heat of summer still a month away—so they had moved outside to eat under the stars.

Susie sat on the top of a picnic bench with her feet resting on the seat, watching as Richard fished out the last morsels of a chocolate shake with a long plastic spoon. *He's overdoing the pretty-boy surfer vibe,* she thought. The Hawaiian shirt and cargo shorts went with his frosted blond hair—but spoiled rich guys with attitude weren't her type. She'd seen her share of self-important rich boys growing up in Guangzhou—boys whose families had money and influence. They didn't have to try because they had everything handed to them.

Susie finished her too-greasy french fries and listened to one side of Doctor Sterling's conversation with the university's science department chair.

"No, that's what I'm telling you. It definitely isn't a meteorite." Doctor Sterling spoke excitedly into his cellphone as he paced outside the Fros-T-Freez. "Did you even look at the pictures I sent?"

Thaddeus Sterling wore a sweat-stained "Schist Happens" T-shirt and tan bucket hat. Engrossed in his phone call, he absent-mindedly brushed at his jeans, which were so worn and covered in sandstone dust they were more red than blue.

"It's human-made. Has to be," he said. A pause. "The sides are too smooth, and the corners are too sharp to be natural, even for a crystalline formation." He spun on his feet and paced in the other direction. "Yes, I thought about that, but this thing was several feet under rock and sand. It showed no sign of any damage."

Another pause.

"Uh-huh. Certainly nothing commercial—we'd have heard about it. Maybe something military? But we haven't found any wreckage. And crashing right in the center of the crater? That's highly improbable. Well, could you at least ask around for me?"

He scratched the stubble on his chin thoughtfully. "I dunno. Maybe another day or so before we can move it to base camp and take a better look."

Doctor Sterling finished his call just as a battered orange- and rust-colored Jeep Rubicon pulled into the parking lot.

"She's all gassed up and ready to head back when you say, Professor," Declan called from the driver's seat. "Richie, I hope you've saved me a burger."

"I told you, it's Richard. No one calls me Richie but my kid sister."

"Aw, lighten up, Richie boy. We're all friends here," Declan said, then shot Susie a wink.

***

Two days later, Declan and Richard went back into town for supplies. As he loaded the last case of bottled water into the battered Jeep, Declan wiped the sweat from his broad forehead with a dusty bandana and returned it to his pocket. Though it was not yet midday, the desert sun was merciless.

"Oy! I'm not makin' too much noise for ya, am I, yer highness?" His Irish brogue became more noticeable when he was irritated.

Richard barely looked up from his cellphone. "Nah, you're fine." He sat in the passenger seat, legs crossed and hanging out the open window.

Climbing behind the wheel with a grunt, Declan switched on the engine and sped away from the City Market onto Moab's only main street. Richard scrambled to get his legs back inside. "What's your problem?"

Declan said nothing as he drove north, then turned toward Canyonlands and their base camp. He wished Susie had volunteered to make this week's supply run instead of Richard. Susie was always pleasant and never minded pitching in to help or getting her hands dirty. Declan didn't like spending any more time with this pompous, rich prick than he had to.

Parked just off the side of the highway, the occupants of a dark SUV watched them intently as they passed.

***

Declan sensed a *wrongness* as they pulled into the camp. It was too quiet. The modest base camp was little more than four sun-faded dome tents and an olive-drab army surplus canopy to store supplies out of the sun. A common area separated their sleeping units—a dining fly hung suspended by aluminum poles over a pair of dusty plastic folding tables and a handful of outdated lawn chairs. Sand sagebrush clung in clumps here and there, with Sonoran scrub oaks and craggy, thirsty junipers providing a few modest patches of shade. Everything else was a desiccated Mars scape of red sand and rocks. Neither Susie nor Professor Sterling was visible anywhere.

Declan and Richard had passed an empty Lincoln parked just off the dirt road a short distance from their base camp. It didn't belong to anyone from their group, which aroused their suspicion. Criminals occasionally targeted campers and hikers, especially this far off the main highway. He quickly scanned the area as he stepped out of the Jeep.

"Sometin' ain't right, Richie boy," he said. "Watch the car whilst I take a look down the hill."

Crossing the open space between their tents, Declan noticed two half-cooked burgers in a pan on the cookstove, its flame unlit. Flies buzzed and landed on the ketchup-slathered buns on the table nearby. Not a good sign. Susie and the professor wouldn't have just left camp in the middle of preparing their lunch.

Declan moved closer to the edge of their camp. A walking trail crisscrossed a steep slope down to the dig site. Ducking under a low branch, he watched Sterling and Susie wrestling with the strange gray object they had unearthed two days before. An unknown man in wraparound sunglasses stood to one side. The man's new jeans and skin-tight black T-shirt looked pristine and out of place, unlike Declan's friends, who were covered in days of dust as they struggled to maneuver the object into a rope carry-harness.

Declan was just about to shout down to them when he saw Mr. Wraparound's gun. Pulling back from the edge, out of sight, he turned toward the Jeep—only to come face-to-face with the barrel of a large black pistol.

"Take it real slow there, Red. Let's see those hands." Another man, this one wearing Ray-Bans, motioned at Declan to move back toward the Jeep. Richard was kneeling by the left front tire, his hands secured behind his back. There was a small cut above

Richard's right eye, and he was staring daggers at the man with the gun. The man raised a radio to his ear and pressed a button.

"I've got Pretty Boy and the Moose secured up here," he said. "You're good to bring the unit up."

Declan felt his face flush. The man swapped his radio for a set of zip-tie restraints he pulled from a back pocket.

Richard tried to stand by leaning on the Jeep and pushing up with his legs. He almost made it but overbalanced and fell onto his left side.

It was all Declan needed. When Mr. Ray-Ban turned, Declan decked him with everything he had. His left fist connected with the man's nose, shattering it along with the expensive sunglasses. He went down like a sack of wet sand, dropping the pistol. Declan wasted no time gathering it and slipping it into his waistband. He pulled the filthy bandana from his pocket, stuffed it into the unconscious man's mouth, and then rolled it onto his stomach. He found the restraints, secured the man's hands, and paused to catch his breath. *Now what?* he thought.

"A little help?" Richard called out weakly, still lying where he had fallen.

"Shit! Sorry," Declan said as he cut Richard's ties with a pocketknife.

"There's another one down there with Susie and the Professor. They'll be up here any minute. Help me drag this arsehole out of sight and sit on him while I figure out what to do next."

"Who are they, and what do they want?" Richard asked.

"What d'ya think? They're after the artifact."

***

Ray-Ban was starting to come around, his moaning and coughing muffled by the dust-filled bandana, which was now held in place with a few feet of packing tape. At least the blood had stopped flowing from his nose. Richard had the good sense to wrap the man's legs with a bungee cord from their supply tent before laying him out of sight behind their camp coolers and crates of canned goods. He knelt over the strange man, ready to hit him if he tried anything.

Susie came into view first, then the Professor. They had the gray object slung in a rope harness between them. Each end of the sling was fixed with padded shoulder straps to lessen the strain of carrying the heavy item. Mr. Wraparound followed them closely, pistol still in hand.

"That's far enough," he said. Unlike his partner, this man's noticeable drawl was clearly from the South. "Set it down here, nice and gentle-like."

The Professor, obviously exhausted, took a half step forward to slacken the harness. The shape tipped slightly and then came to rest on the sand between them. He and Susie slipped off their straps. He bent over with his hands on his knees, struggling to catch his breath.

Susie turned to face Mr. Wraparound, her small hands balled into fists, arms at her sides. She was seething. "Chī wǒ de shǐ, nǐ zhè ge hún dàn!" she said.

"Wow, you've got quite a mouth on you for such a tiny thing," the man said, amused. "Zài nǐ zhīhòu, jìnǚ." Susie went quiet. "Didn't expect me to speak Chinese, huh?"

"No, it's not that," she said as Declan brought the pistol down forcefully on the man's head, knocking him out cold.

***

Chapter 2

Declan turned out the two men's pockets. He and Richard had secured them with their hands behind their backs and seated them at the base of the sturdiest juniper tree in the vicinity. Neither had any identification or badges. He suspected these men were mercenaries—hired thugs sent to do the dirty work of stealing the object for someone with money.

The object wasn't a meteorite—they didn't know what it was—but maybe the money man didn't know that. A sizeable meteorite could bring quite a payday, though probably not enough to make it worth hurting or killing someone.

Mr. Ray-Ban had almost one hundred dollars in cash and the keys to a Lincoln Navigator. It was likely the black SUV he and Richard had passed earlier. Declan pocketed the wad of bills and threw the keys as far as he could out into the sagebrush, not caring where they landed. Pulling out the pistol he'd taken from Mr. Wraparound, he squatted and leaned close to the two men.

"Who are you working for?" he said.

Mr. Wraparound was still groggy—or feigning it. Ray-Ban kept his eyes forward and fixed on nothing.

"You've made a big mistake," he said coolly. He looked down and spat blood on Declan's shoe.

"Funny, I could probably say the same to you by the look of yer face," Declan said. "I asked you a question, arsehole."

No reply.

"Fine," Declan said. "Have it your way." He looked up, shading his eyes. "Sunset's not for several hours yet, and this sad tree won't do much for shade. I'm guessin' the two of you are going to get mighty thirsty before you manage to free yourselves, and I'm afraid we'll be takin' all the water with us. You never can be too careful in the desert."

Declan made a show of almost finishing a water bottle, then made a satisfying "Ah" sound and smacked his lips. He rinsed the blood off his shoe with the remaining water, then dropped the empty bottle into the man's lap—spilling the last few drops—as he rose to his feet and moved toward the Jeep with the others.

"Oh, and even if you find those keys, Richie here tells me your Lincoln ain't goin' anywhere," Declan said, glancing back. "You should probably see if your tire warranty covers payback punctures."

"Damn it, Declan, I told you, it's *Richard.*"

***

The old Jeep drove for a half-mile, dodging arroyos and large rocks. Declan navigated the treacherous terrain northward at a snail's pace before he felt safe to reenter the highway. They had strapped the strange object in the back under a plastic tarp.

Richard rode shotgun—in this case, an accurate description—they had liberated a pump-action twelve-gauge and several boxes of ammunition from the black SUV. Susie rode in the back with Doctor Sterling, who didn't look well. He hadn't spoken since they'd left the site. She was pretty sure it was heatstroke brought on by the exertion of hauling their find into camp at gunpoint. She was younger and in better shape—yet she was frazzled as well.

Susie removed the washcloth from Sterling's forehead and wrung it out. She reapplied cool water from a plastic bottle before replacing it, then gently took his wrist and checked his pulse.

"How's he doing?" Richard said, viewing them in the rear-view mirror with genuine concern.

"I think his pulse is back to near normal," she replied. "The cool compress and getting him out of the sun helped. A lot."

Declan followed the highway east toward Moab. They planned to file a report at the sheriff's office and maybe try to get some answers. Someone had taken notice of their find, and not in a good way. He wondered if it was the Professor's call two nights ago to Doctor Price at the university—and if Price had asked the wrong questions or if it went deeper. Was someone tracking them and listening to their phones? Declan and Richard scrutinized every passing vehicle while simultaneously watching for any trouble following in their wake.

The Jeep slowed at the sheriff's station but didn't stop. Like many of the buildings lining the main street, the small one-story structure hadn't changed much since the early part of the last century. Once painted a deep red, the brick facade had chipped and faded to a dull terra-cotta from decades in the desert sun. Two late-model black SUVs sat in front, looking eerily like the Lincoln they had disabled at the dig site. In this small rural town, the shiny new vehicles were conspicuously inconspicuous. Sitting in the battered orange Jeep, Declan disliked how exposed he felt. His prior smugness had all but evaporated.

Doctor Sterling spoke up at last.

"Declan, turn around. I don't know what's happening, but I have a feeling this may be more complicated than we think."

Declan waited for a break in traffic, then headed north—back the way they had come. They approached an alley that cut through a row of older buildings converted to shops. The narrow roadway led behind a vegan-run hipster clothing shop and a mountain bike mechanic.

"Pull in there off the street while we figure out what to do next," he said.

They watched from the alley as yet another unmarked black vehicle cruised south toward the sheriff's station.

"What's happening, Professor?" Richard asked. "Who are these people, the FBI? Why are they after us?"

"I don't think it's the FBI," said Sterling. "I had my suspicions that the device might be military in origin, but if that were the case, why all the cloak and dagger? They could just show up and demand that we turn it over. No, these guys may want it badly enough, but they don't have a legitimate claim. At least nothing they're willing to bring under any scrutiny. If Declan hadn't gotten the drop on those two—"

He was cut off by a cacophony of sounds emanating from their phones in unison. Richard was the first to pull up his screen. As he read the text, all color drained from his face.

"It—It's an Amber Alert," he yelped as his eyes swept the Jeep's interior. He turned the screen for the others to see. "They're looking for *us*."

AMBER ALERT - Grand County Sheriff's Office

Victim is Trina Matheson, age 6, from Page, AZ.

Abducted near Canyonlands NP - Islands in the Sky Visitor Ctr.

Suspect vehicle: Orange 2009 Jeep Rubicon, UT plate #RD5-03Y

Last known location - Moab area - if seen, call 911

"Who the hell is Trina Matheson?" Susie asked.

"I doubt she exists," said Doctor Sterling. "Someone is either working with or using the sheriff to get to us."

"Well, Professor," Declan said, "What d'ye suggest we do now?"

"Whoever these guys are, they obviously have connections," Richard said. "Still, if we put our phones in airplane mode and switch them off, I don't think they'll be able to track them."

"That might buy us some time," Sterling said, "but to do what, I don't know."

Declan furrowed his brow as he scanned the shops' back lots and loading areas. With its cluttered stacks of old crates, pallets, and assorted junk accumulated over decades, the alley was a far cry from the freshly painted tourist-facing facades along Main Street. Behind the Castle Rock florist shop, a beat-up old van was backed against the roll-up door.

"I think I might have an idea."

***

They stopped for gas at a quaint mom-and-pop station north of town, then drove the interstate east toward Colorado.

The white Ford van was older than their Jeep, but Declan hoped it would be less noticeable. He also hoped the florist wouldn't notice it missing and file a report until Monday, giving them time to put some distance between themselves and whoever was after the strange object.

After forty-five minutes, Richard said, "Declan, find a rest stop. I have to pee."

"I told you not to get that damn fifty-five-gallon drum of soda," Declan scolded. "Besides, we're makin' good time."

"It's called a *Big Swig*," Richard said. "And it was cheaper than the twenty-ounce bottle."

They pulled into a rest area near the state line, and Richard and Susie took advantage of the facilities. Declan backed the van into a parking space near the exit, ready to take off at a moment's notice. He watched the stretch of highway intently, but no one followed them. Sterling pulled out his cellphone, switched it on, and scrolled through his address book.

"Are you sure that's a good idea, Professor?" Declan asked, glancing back. "What if they're trackin' our phones?"

"We'll know for sure one way or another," Sterling said. He hit the autodial and placed the phone against his ear.

"Thelonious, it's Dad. Listen, I'm in some trouble—and I need your help." He spoke quickly, knowing there was a good chance someone was listening.

As he finished the call, Susie and Richard climbed in and slid the side door shut with a loud *clang!* Declan started the van and prepared to pull out toward the highway.

"Wait," Sterling said, stepping out and walking toward an ancient pickup with New Mexico plates. He glanced around, then quickly rummaged through several dog-eared boxes piled near the back of the bed. With another quick look, he turned and reentered the van. Declan regarded him questioningly before heading east down the interstate with a shrug.

***

The *Settle Inn* had the distinction of being the only motel in Olathe, Colorado, which wasn't much of a distinction at all. It was little more than a two-story collection of cinder blocks held together by decades of alternating layers of beige, off-white, and tan paint.

Eighteen identical green doors—nine up, nine down—faced a cracked parking lot that probably hadn't seen fresh asphalt since Reagan was in the White House.

A blue-haired woman behind the counter adjusted her gaudy rhinestone-studded glasses. A string of fake pearls hung from each side and wrapped behind her shriveled neck. She traced her skeletal finger through the guest registry that sat open on the counter in front of her.

"No, nobody has checked in under any of the names you gave me," she said.

The *Jeopardy!* theme song blared from a TV in the manager's apartment behind her, and a thick haze of acrid cigarette smoke hung about a foot from the ceiling. The run-down motel was just off the highway. Yet, based on the number of cars parked out front, it currently housed only half a dozen or so guests. Beneath the yellowed NO SMOKING placard near the entrance, an ancient neon VACANCY sign in the window buzzed angrily.

The woman pulled her glasses off and let them drop to her sagging bosom. She warily eyed the man in front of the counter, who was obviously agitated and having a terrible day from the looks of him. He smelled like he hadn't showered in a week. Blood seeped from a bandage across the bridge of his nose, and he had the beginnings of two black eyes.

"Don't you keep electronic records?" he said, exasperated. He glanced around for a computer. "Do you check IDs when you book a room?"

"Sure, if they want to use a credit card," she said, tapping the ancient flatbed card imprinter on the counter. "No reason to if they pay cash up front."

Thaddeus Sterling's phone had tripped an alert when it pinged a cell tower in Grand Junction. *The old guy must have forgotten to switch it off after they left the rest stop,* the man thought. They apparently turned south because there was another hit in Delta. In the last two hours, the trackers had registered several pings from a tower just half a mile away from this motel. None of them had acquaintances or relatives in this area. This motel was the only logical place they could be.

"Did anyone check in and pay with cash in the last three hours?"

She pulled her glasses back on and slowly traced her finger through the registry again.

"Well, a Mr. Silver checked in at five o'clock. Paid cash for one night. He only wrote down two guests, though. Just him and his wife, I guess. He's in room four."

Mr. Ray-Ban—or Steve Bronsky—was out the door before she could look up.

***

Steve kicked the door open with enough force to embed the security chain into the drywall near the doorframe. The top hinge separated, and the cheap wooden door sagged under its own weight. He quickly stepped inside with his gun drawn.

"Hands where I can see them!" he shouted.

The older couple making love in the room screamed in unison, the woman toppling to one side of the bed and onto the floor with a *thud.* She frantically grasped at the blanket to cover herself. The man sat up, eyes wide and fixed on the pistol. His hands shot up immediately.

"I didn't know she was married, mister. Honest," he said.

They had to be in their eighties.

Steve quickly scanned the room, then dropped his aim and holstered his gun. As he turned to leave, he said, "Don't worry, grandpa. Your secret's safe with me."

Jesus, he thought. *I'll need to wash my eyes out with bleach to unsee that.*

***

Declan parked the van in a dark corner of the underground lot, and the four of them boarded the elevator to the Sixteenth Street mall above. Most of the shops were closed or closing at this hour, but the restaurants were open and bustling with customers.

They made their way to a Western-themed bar and grill at the north end of the main building and shuffled past patrons waiting for tables. Dark-stained wooden walls surrounded the space; ambient droplights hung suspended over each table. Hank Williams crooned "Your Cheatin' Heart" from a vintage-looking jukebox just right of the bar. Waitresses crisscrossed the restaurant in uniforms a mix of Daisy Duke and the Dallas Cowboy Cheerleaders.

At a booth near the back wall, a man who looked remarkably like Doctor Sterling—albeit twenty-five years younger—waved to them as they approached.

"Susie, Richard, Declan, this is my son, Thelonious," Doctor Sterling said as they slid into the booth. Declan nodded, immediately and unceremoniously attacking the remaining hot wings in the center of the table.

"Why Thelonious?" Richard asked.

"His mother and I were big fans of eclectic Jazz music and especially Thelonious Monk," Doctor Sterling said. "He passed away when we were expecting our son, so we decided to name him Thelonious."

"Just call me Theo," the younger man said, grinning. "No one calls me Thelonious"—he shot his dad a look—"unless I'm in trouble."

"Well, Thelonious," said Richard, "I think you just joined the Big Trouble Club."

***

Chapter 3

Theo's lab was in CU Denver's Experimental Physics building, not far from downtown. The modern steel and glass structure—newer than most other campus buildings—stood on the university's northernmost end. Theo parked his BMW in his reserved space, then joined the others.

"What the hell is it?" Theo said as they stood near the rear of the van. He leaned in for a closer look, and a mild wave of nausea overtook him. He took a half step back, eyeing the object warily.

"If I knew that, we wouldn't have driven halfway across Colorado," Thaddeus said. "You're the physicist. Why don't you tell me what it is?"

"Let's get it inside—I have some equipment that might help. First classes aren't until eleven on Monday, so we'll have the place to ourselves the rest of the weekend."

"Lead the way, Prof—er...Theo," Declan said.

Theo retrieved a wheeled cart from inside the building. As they lifted the object onto it, Richard looked uneasy.

"Doctor Sterling, I think the magnetic field is increasing," he said.

"It feels more noticeable than when we moved it from the Jeep in Moab."

"I noticed that, too," Theo said. "I have a gauss meter inside. We should be able to put a number to it."

Richard and Declan pushed the cart up a short ramp and through the exterior doors while the older Doctor Sterling and Susie brought the bags with their personal gear. A bright green tarp shielded the object (the pseudo-sphere, as Theo called it) from any prying eyes. They needn't have worried, though, as the halls were empty given the late hour. Every sound seemed to ricochet off the walls and increase in volume. Declan checked the time; it was just past midnight. He found it hard to believe that only twelve hours had passed since the physical confrontation with the two strange men and their hurried exodus from the dig site.

"This is my lab up ahead—to the right," said Theo.

He hurried to scan his ID badge at an electronic box near the set of double doors. A bar across the top lit up in bright green, and the door unlocked with a high-pitched *beep!* They pushed the cart through and into the large room.

Declan turned three-hundred-sixty degrees, taking in the chaotic lab space. Some of the items were recognizable to any college student who'd spent time in a chemistry or biology lab—the chemical fume hoods against the back wall, for example—but others may as well have come from the set of a Frankenstein movie remake. Brightly colored hoses of both flammable and inert gasses hung alongside power cords at regular intervals from the ceiling. Some were attached to strange devices mounted to workstations, and others were waiting to be of use. Shiny, pristine-looking, newer technology sat alongside items with worn wooden cases that might have been in use since the 60s. Along one side of the room stood a stack of recently unpacked metal shipping crates. Susie dropped the two large bags she was shouldering and turned to Theo.

"Which way to the, uh, restrooms?" she asked.

Theo gestured with his hand. "Back through the doors, then right to the end of the hall. The last two doors before you turn the corner. You can't miss them."

She turned to go but stopped and said, "How will I be able to get back in here?"

Theo tossed her his badge, and she caught it by the attached lanyard.

"Keep it in your pocket. Don't let anyone see my photo on that, or someone might start asking some uncomfortable questions."

Susie nodded, then turned to go. Theo moved across the open room and pushed a large device mounted on a wheeled table toward where the others had placed the strange gray object.

"Alright, my precious," he said in a strange Golem-like voice. "Let's find out what you're made of."

***

As she stepped out of the complex's rear exit, Susie pulled up her contacts list and hit the speed dial. The person on the other end answered after only one ring. A woman's voice, clearly agitated, spoke in unbroken Mandarin as Susie listened, trying to get a word in. Finally, the woman on the other end relented—*or ran out of oxygen,* Susie thought—and allowed her to explain why she hadn't checked in sooner. Susie explained what she could, promised to stay in contact if possible, then made her excuses and disconnected the call—making sure to reengage the phone's prior setting before returning it to her purse. She scanned Theo's badge and moved quickly past the restrooms toward the lab.

***

X-ray fluorescence failed to identify the alloy used to construct the object. The readout showed no fluorescence present, which had to be an error. Theo had checked it twice before swapping it for a death-ray-looking device suspended from a wheeled tripod.

"Laser emission spectroscopy should give us a clearer picture of the object's composition," he said. "Unfortunately, there's a good chance it will scorch or mar the surface."

Thaddeus thought for a moment before responding. "We need answers, son. That's a risk we'll have to live with."

Theo positioned the device with its aperture aimed at the center of one of the pentagonal facets. He passed around sets of amber-tinted safety glasses, not wanting to be responsible for any injury from the argon laser. Once everyone had donned their glasses and stepped behind the LES module, Theo took hold of the triggering device attached by a length of cable.

"All ready?" he asked, seeing the group nod.

Theo pressed the button, and the laser switched on, humming loudly with the amount of power consumed. The concentrated beam struck the center of the depression in the facet closest to them. Theo's brow wrinkled, and he turned to look at the LED screen attached to the unit.

"No, that's not right," he said. "That can't ..."

The laser's hum increased in volume and appeared to pick up an infrasound element that they felt rather than heard.

"Something's wrong," Theo said. He switched off the laser and moved to wheel the unit away from the object when Thaddeus grabbed his shoulder forcefully. Then he realized he could still feel the low vibration, and the hum he had thought was coming from the laser was still increasing—and was instead being produced by the strange object on the table before them.

The LES module began to move forward slowly until it came to rest against the object. Richard looked nauseated; in fact, he was practically green. They all were starting to feel the adverse effect.

Across the room from them, the empty shipping crates shifted, then toppled. The hum grew louder still.

"Look!" Susie said, loud enough to be heard above the growing noise. She pointed to the overhead lights, which had begun to sway slightly. The hoses and electric cables swung about like snakes trapped in the ceiling tiles.

The light increased in intensity, matching the sound volume emitted by the strange device. Thaddeus removed his safety glasses and noticed all the depressions in the object had begun to glow with deep purplish light, almost ultraviolet. The hairs on his arms were standing on end.

"We need to leave—now!"

Theo quickly ushered them toward the door. Before they reached the exit, a blinding blue-white light flashed behind them. Thaddeus briefly saw their shadows starkly outlined on the wall ahead, and then everything went black.

For several miles in every direction, downtown Denver and its surrounding neighborhoods were plunged into darkness as the power grid experienced an unprecedented cascading failure.

***

The *Starlite Diner* hearkened back to a bygone age with its red and white Naugahyde seats, checkerboard tile floor, and chrome everything else. Reproductions of gold records and autographed photos of Elvis, Little Richard, and Buddy Holly emulated the look and feel of 1950s Americana. A short-order cook in a plain white T-shirt and paper hat labored at the grill behind the counter, his bright blue hair and lip piercings an anachronistic affront to the overall atmosphere.

Steve Bronsky sat in a corner booth near the window, a half-eaten western omelet on the table in front of him. He scrolled through his phone's recent messages, then peered outside for what felt like the hundredth time. His agitation grew with each passing minute as he waited for his partner.

"More coffee, hon?"

Startled, Steve glanced up as the smiling waitress materialized as if from nowhere and refilled his cup, not bothering to wait for an answer. She glided away, topping off the rest of her early morning customers on her way back toward the counter. The sound of sleigh bells rattling against the metal doorframe pulled Steve's attention back toward the front entrance. *Finally,* he thought.

The two men served together in Kabul until an IED took out Nate's Humvee, and he was sent home to recover from his injuries. Later, they were reunited at the NSA when Tomlinson hand-selected them for his Black Eagles team.

Nate Travers strolled over, casually taking the seat across the table as he eyed his partner's battered face. Both of Steve's eyes were blackened now; deep purple bruises spread above his cheekbones and into the corners of his eyes. The bandage across the bridge of his nose was fresh, but the flesh beneath it was angry and discolored.

"Man, you look like shit," Nate joked, trying to keep his grin in check. His lilting southern accent somehow made Steve more irritated with the man. "Even worse than yesterday, if that's even possible."

"How's your head, *Goober*?" Steve said with a scowl.

Nate's smile slipped from his face as he reached back gingerly to the lump at the base of his skull.

"You know I hate when you call me that, Bronsky," he said. "It's not my fault you got sucker-punched by that Irish fuck. You never shoulda taken your eyes off him."

"If I recall," Steve said dryly, "he got the drop on you too."

"You gonna finish that?"

Changing the subject, Nate pulled Steve's breakfast toward himself. He dug into it with gusto, grinning at his partner while stuffing a large forkful into his mouth.

The waitress appeared as if from nowhere, pouring a steaming cup of coffee and sliding it in front of Nate, who gave her a half nod. Steve placed his hand over his own cup before she could refill it.

"No more for me," he said. He watched as Nate polished off the last of the omelet. "Just give him the check. We need to get moving."

Nate tried to protest through a mouthful of egg and cheese, but Steve was already halfway out the door.

***

"We got a hit on Yang Shu's cell," Nate said as they drove through downtown Denver. They passed several power utility trucks—men in buckets trying to find the cause of the previous night's blackout.

"Turns out she was at the university when the power went down around midnight."

"Or at least *her phone* was," corrected Steve. He thought back to the incident at the motel the day before and shuddered. He was sure he would be fired—or worse—for that screw-up. Tomlinson had chewed both their asses up one side and down the other for nearly an hour.

"Security cameras picked her up by the physics building's loading dock, talking on the phone. There's no audio—but it's definitely her," Nate said. "She used a badge to get inside. The power outage happened about ten minutes later."

Nate parked the Camry on the street half a block from the physics building, and the pair got out. The Grand County sheriff had arranged for a flatbed tow truck for their Lincoln. With no other agency vehicle available, they had rented the Camry to pursue the lead on the group outside of Grand Junction. Nate had found Sterling's phone tucked into a box of spare parts in the older man's pickup in the *Settle Inn* parking lot.

The two men approached the main building and noted the *Castle Rock Florist* van in the visitor lot. A uniformed officer was standing at the main entrance, but whatever was happening inside had his attention. Nate kept an eye on him while Steve peered in the rear windows.

"Empty," he said.

They flashed their credentials to the beat cop at the door, then moved inside. At the end of the hall, a couple of FBI types gave themselves away with their impeccable suits and matching ties and pocket squares. These were probably only local agents, and Steve didn't see anyone he recognized. As they approached, one of the men blocked their path.

"I'm sorry, gentlemen. This is an active investigation," he said.

Nate and Steve exchanged a look, then produced their ID in unison. The agent scrutinized the credentials and then took a closer look at both men.

"Why are *you* here? This was called in as a possible bombing," he said.

"And...?" Nate raised an eyebrow.

"And there's no sign of explosives, no bomb residue, no combustible material of any kind. It appears a student may have been conducting a physics experiment that went off the rails in some way. We're still trying to connect the dots."

Steve said, "What do you mean *off the rails,* agent...?"

"Baker," the man said. "Perhaps you should see for yourselves."

He ushered them inside. The lab did indeed appear to be a bomb site. Every corner of the big room had equipment forcefully shoved into it. Gauges and LED screens were cracked and broken. There was not an intact piece of glass in the room.

"It's fortunate this is an inside room with no windows," said agent Baker.

"Yes, most fortunate," said Nate, unable to mask his sarcasm.

He and Steve continued to scan the wrecked lab for the strange object—under the guise of assessing the carnage—but it was becoming apparent it was not there. Nate suspected the artifact *had* been there at some point, and likely it had caused all of *this* somehow.

The white ceiling tiles were crushed and in pieces everywhere. Near the center of the room, several floor tiles showed stress fractures, as if someone had dropped a great weight on them.

"Nate, what do you make of this?" Steve asked. He pointed back toward the exit.

Neither man had noticed it when they had entered because their focus had been directed *into* the room. Now Nate could see a distinct discoloration on the wall just inside the double doors. It looked like a shadow of sorts, but the image was lighter than the surrounding walls. He could make out several overlapping silhouettes—as if four or five people were moving toward the door when...whatever happened.

Nate reached out his hand and touched the shape. It was smooth, almost glossy. The paint outside it, however, was dull. When he touched it, a layer like fine ash flaked off.

"Did you test this?" he asked agent Baker.

The man just stood dumbfounded. "There were people in here during the incident?" he said. "How did they survive all of this"—he gestured to the room—" and where are they now?"

"That, my friend, is the million-dollar question," said Steve.

***

Chapter 4

Steve and Nate watched over agent Baker's shoulder as the images paraded across his laptop. The timestamp in the lower-left corner indicated the time of the video was just past midnight—00:06, local time. The wide-angle lens distorted the view slightly, but the sacrificed image quality was offset by the larger area captured by the cameras. The university hadn't sprung for high-end equipment—crime was relatively low in this area of town. They had added these security cameras nearly a decade ago as an afterthought, using donor money set aside for campus upgrades.

At 00:08, the white florist van pulled up, then backed in near the wheelchair ramp adjacent to the front steps. Four individuals exited the vehicle. Steve recognized the giant bearded driver almost immediately and scowled.

"That's them," he said. "No question about it."

They watched as a moment later, a large, gray BMW X7 pulled past and parked in a reserved space opposite. A black man in his forties stepped out and moved toward the others.

"Who's that?" asked agent Baker.

"That's Doctor Sterling," Nate said. "The *younger* Doctor Sterling. He's a physics professor here. It was his lab that got trashed last night."

The man stepped out of view, and the image split. The right half of the screen now showed the entrance from above.

"These are motion activated?" Steve asked.

"Looks like it," said Baker.

A moment later, young Doctor Sterling reappeared with a flatbed cart. The three younger men transferred something large and heavy to the cart, a plastic tarp obscuring it from the camera's watchful gaze. The readout at the bottom read 00:12 as they pushed the item through the double doors.

"The feed ends there," Baker said. "No one else enters or leaves via this exit until the power outage at twelve fifty-two."

"What time did Yang exit the loading dock?" Steve said.

Baker's eyes narrowed. "How did you know about *that*? We only pulled the video an hour ago."

"Just run it," Steve said.

Agent baker clicked on a second icon, and the video feed from the back of the building came up. They watched as the small Asian woman moved several feet away from the building, looked back over her shoulder, then pulled out a cellphone at 00:37. She spoke hurriedly, glancing back repeatedly.

"I'm guessing she didn't clear this call with the others, based on her body language," Nate said. "Why would she risk it after they went through so much trouble to throw us off their trail?"

"She's in the US on a student visa—no family outside of Guangzhou. Maybe her family keeps close tabs on her," said Steve.

"Maybe," said Nate. Something about her body language was still off, though.

"OK, so, twelve-forty-one, she wraps up the call and heads back in," said agent Baker. "Card ID was registered to Thelonious Sterling, according to security's records."

They watched as she held out an access badge, scanned it, and reentered the building.

"And eleven minutes later, all hell breaks loose inside," said Nate. "What time did they leave the building?"

"Unknown," Baker said. "Power cut at twelve-fifty-two, emergency backup power kicked on almost immediately. The cameras—actually, the PCs they're connected to—took just over two minutes to reboot. There is no recorded footage until the local police showed up nine minutes later responding to the automatic alarm and found the place empty."

"There's no campus security?" asked Steve.

"CU Denver is one of three universities in what is called Auraria campus. They share a police force with the state college and community college. They're a small force, and it was on a weekend night. Not much happening on campus," Baker said.

Nate thought back through the video and its associated timeline. It had taken them four minutes to unload the device and wheel it inside, plus probably at least a couple to unload it in the lab. No way they could have done the reverse in only two minutes. And the empty van hadn't moved from where they'd parked it the night before.

"Is that BMW still in the stall out front?" he asked.

Baker nodded slowly.

***

A search of Thelonious Sterling's home turned up nothing. Steve was careful to replace every book, box, and paper precisely as he found it. He hadn't bothered to go through the process of obtaining a search warrant for a couple of reasons.

The first was that any judge would require probable cause, and he had nothing he could divulge to the local authorities. The second reason was that his superiors had made it clear that any unauthorized agency exposure would have him riding a desk for the foreseeable future.

Although he was wearing gloves, he still wiped every surface behind himself as he went, taking care not to leave any trace behind.

Nate pulled the Camry into the small access road that ran behind the house. Trash cans were lined up neatly along the length of the alleyway, waiting for the next pickup. Steve slipped through a side gate and climbed into the passenger side. At the next corner, Nate turned and drove toward their motel.

"Nothing there," Steve said. "It doesn't look like he has been here since Friday morning."

The agency had provided them with Thelonious's phone records, and they confirmed he received the call from his father Friday afternoon. Facial recognition run on security footage from the Sixteenth Street mall showed Thelonious Sterling arrived separately from the others, who showed up around the time Steve was kicking in a hotel room door almost three-hundred miles away.

By the time they figured out the ruse, the group was already either at or headed to CU Denver. Since early Saturday morning, there had been no sign of anyone from the group.

The agency was combing through every bit of footage from security cameras throughout the metro Denver area but so far had failed to turn up anything useful.

With few exceptions, any camera that captured digital files and uploaded them to the cloud was fair game—including ATM cameras and video doorbells. Certain officials at HSI and the NSA had seen the benefit of millions of cameras capturing images and video twenty-four seven. They ensured that they had encrypted back door access covertly installed in every commercial video device produced in the last ten years.

Nate's phone buzzed, and he handed it to Steve. He hadn't taken the time to set up the hands-free feature in the rental car.

"Go ahead," said Steve, engaging the external speaker.

"It's agent Baker. We have preliminary lab results back on the paint from the lab."

"Let me guess," Nate said. "It's been oxidized."

"Not exactly," Baker said. "It's been chemically altered at a molecular level."

"What the hell does that mean?" Steve chimed in.

"The physics building is less than ten years old. For the past decade, the university has made a public show of reducing its carbon footprint and making decisions it deems eco-friendly," Baker said. "Recycled building materials, Earth-friendly paint, etc."

"So, the organic materials in the paint are gone, leaving the pigment and a few odd ingredients behind," Nate said.

"Have your team see if anything else organic is missing from the lab and let us know ASAP—anything, no matter how insignificant it seems. You got me?"

"We're already on it. In addition to the paint, the ceiling tiles show the same type of alteration. That's part of why they are so fragile—more than half of their mass is just...gone."

Steve covered the phone mouthpiece with his hand. "What do you think it means?" he asked.

"I don't know for sure yet," Nate said. "But it may begin to explain why we didn't find our scientists laid out in the wreckage of the lab. What it doesn't explain is what *did* happen to them."

***

Jordan Baker leafed through the report for a second time, still trying to put the puzzle pieces together. Feeling the beginnings of a nagging headache, he pinched the bridge of his nose and squeezed his eyes shut. Against his better judgment—but not wanting to make waves with HSI—Baker had called Travers and Bronsky and arranged to meet with them in his office. He glanced at his watch. They should be here any minute.

As if on cue, there was a short double knock at his door.

"It's open," Baker said.

The two men walked in, each taking a seat across the desk from him.

"Well, you said it was important," Nate said. "What have you got?"

Baker set the sheaf of papers on the desk and turned them so the pair could read them. Nate scanned the first page, then handed it to Bronsky as he moved to the next.

"Empty soup cans? *That's* why you called us here?" Nate said incredulously.

"*Unopened* empty soup cans," said Baker. "And these."

He reached into a box and produced a couple of fast-food bags, their tops folded over with receipts stapled in the center, and two Hershey chocolate bars.

"The techs are still processing the soup cans. We found them in a drawer with the candy bars. Probably one of the students or Sterling himself kept them around for a quick lunch." Baker said. "I keep a couple of ramen cups in my desk for the same reason. These"—he pushed the bags toward the two men—"were found when we moved some of the lab furniture to collect other samples. Look at the date."

Nate lifted one of the two bags, surprised by its lightness. The attached receipt was from 11:46 the previous evening.

"They must have stopped on their way to the lab," Steve said, picking up the other bag. He noticed the Burger Heaven logo. "This place is just a few blocks from there."

Someone had opened the bag. Steve peered in to see empty fry boxes, napkins, and burger wrappers. The foil was smooth, not wrinkled, as if it still contained the sandwiches. There was also not a crumb of french fry in the bag.

"I don't get it," he said finally. "Why dump everything out, then go to so much trouble rearranging the packaging?"

"That's just it," said Baker. "Our technicians opened the bags. Everything is just how they found them. Also, there's not a speck of ketchup or cheese in the wrappers—no grease. Have you ever seen something like that? There was no food or food waste in the trash, either. Then there are the chocolate bars."

He pushed those forward, and Nate noticed something he hadn't before. These foil pouches appeared factory sealed at both ends—yet the candy inside seemed to have evaporated.

Nate looked at the list on the report's last page. In addition to the paint, the ceiling tiles, the items on the desk, and the soup cans, it listed three potted plants—and every ounce of potting soil. They had found the empty pots lined up on top of a bookcase near the back wall. All organic materials in a twenty-foot radius from the lab's center had gone missing, along with five scientists and one very curious, very significant artifact.

***

Chapter 5

Theo rolled onto his side, shivering from the cold. He opened his eyes but couldn't seem to bring the world into focus. His head was pounding, and every inch of his body hurt. He was outside—the lab was *gone.* He tried to sit up but only managed to raise himself on one elbow in the dirt. *Dirt?* He tried to take in his surroundings, but his rational mind could not properly process the scene. One minute, he was running toward the door, trying to put distance between them and the strange object. There was a flash—an explosion, he assumed—and he was thrown forward and off his feet. He didn't remember anything after that. *Probably a concussion,* he thought. *And somehow, I ended up...on Mars?*

"Theo, are you alright?" Thaddeus's voice rang out somewhere behind him.

Theo tried to raise his arm but found he was too weak. He couldn't see where the sound was coming from. Declan stepped over toward him and looked down, concerned.

"Over here, Professor," he called out. Leaning closer, he said, "Can you stand? Is anythin' broken?"

Theo tried to speak but could only manage a weak whisper.

"Is this...Mars?"

Declan let out a deep, bellowing laugh.

"I think Theo may be delirious, Professor. He thinks he's on Mars!"

Thaddeus made his way over to where his son was now sitting upright. He reached out a hand to help him up. When Theo had gotten to his feet, he put an arm around his shoulder to steady him. Theo could now see Susie and Richard looking into a deep depression about ten feet away.

"It's not Mars," Thaddeus said, "but it might as well be. We somehow traveled over two hundred and fifty miles in an impossibly short time. I don't know how long we've been here. It seems we all lost consciousness. Susie and Richard were the first to come around, then Declan, and then me. And then you. You were the closest to the device when ..." He trailed off—a pensive, troubled look on his face.

They began walking toward the others. Theo gradually gained his balance, and his headache subsided. The sun was now reaching the crater floor where they stood, chasing away the cold of the desert night. His shoe slipped in something wet, and he looked down. At first, he thought someone had been sick. Then he saw two unwrapped chocolate bars beginning to melt in the sun, and a sudden understanding washed over him like a tsunami. The mess on his shoe was a combination of split pea with ham and vegetable beef soup. He glanced around further and saw a small pile of cheeseburgers and french fries lying on the desert sand. To his left, three wilted philodendrons sprawled on the ground, roots partially exposed. The soil that once provided protection and nourishment lay beneath them in disarranged piles. Odd bits of flotsam and jetsam littered the space around them. Theo struggled to process what he was seeing.

When they reached the edge of the depression—which he could now see was a hole scooped out from the crater floor—Theo saw the strange gray device sitting at the bottom, seemingly undamaged. A metallic lab table lay crushed beneath it.

He turned toward his father, eyes wide with disbelief.

"Yeah, I know," Thaddeus said. "But as I said yesterday, you're the physicist. You tell me."

***

"Barring any other empirical evidence, we must form our hypothesis on the observations available to us," Theo said to the group.

"Oy, Theo. Wind yer neck in. I think we all know how the scientific method works," said Declan.

"Right, I know. Sorry," Theo said, embarrassed.

"I'm used to instructing undergrads—it's a hard habit to break, I guess. What I'm saying is this: Do we know—or can we at least postulate—that the device somehow transported us along with an odd assortment of items from my lab into the middle of nowhere? Why here? Why only the soup, but not the cans? Why the food, but not the containers?" He gestured toward the plants. "Why those, but not the pots? None of the tables, chairs, or other items closer to the object made the trip. Why?"

"One of the tables came with us," Richard reminded him. He pointed toward the object and the crushed table beneath it.

"Okay, so why that one?" Theo said. "What's the pattern?"

"Aside from the table, everything else is organic," said Susie.

"But there were items made of wood in the lab," said Richard. "And the food containers would be paper and cardboard. Those are also organic."

Thaddeus had a particular look about him when he was close to a solution, but it remained tantalizingly out of reach.

"We—I mean the US—we don't have anything like that. The technology just doesn't exist," Theo said.

"So, I think we have to confront the elephant in the room—or in this case, the crater."

He gestured toward the device still resting in the shallow hole.

"We didn't build it. I doubt the Chinese or Russians did, either. No one has this capability, or we'd have heard about it. You can't keep something that world-changing a secret, not with a twenty-four-seven media cycle. Groups like Wikileaks and others would find a way to get this out there. You said this crater was millions of years old—"

"Over a hundred million, but yeah," Richard said.

"So... over a hundred million years ago, something crashed here possessing technology that even our modern world can't hope to produce," Theo said. "Something alien." He looked at each of them, letting his words sink in. "I'm starting to see why those guys want this so bad. This is batshit crazy stuff. I'd never have believed it if I didn't experience it myself. Hell, I'm still not sure I believe it. I don't know, Dad. Maybe we should turn it over to them. I feel like we're in over our heads...Dad?"

He turned to look at Thaddeus, who stood near the edge of the hole, only half listening as he surveyed the scene around them. He was still trying to discern some pattern to what they had all experienced.

"The device ended up exactly where we found it," he said, "if you ignore the table. We've all been here before, but Theo hasn't. There's nothing out of place beyond a certain radius of the device. Everything here was in the lab in relative proximity." He turned to Theo. "It all started when you turned the laser onto the device. The concentrated light energy switched it on and activated it. The low hum we all heard and felt must have been the creation of an electromagnetic field or something along those lines."

"I think it started before that, Doctor Sterling," Richard said.

He told them in detail about the itching, crawling feeling he'd had as they moved the device to the cart. Theo commented that he, too, had felt a wave of nausea or unease when he leaned into the van to look at the device for the first time.

"I felt something similar in Moab, but it was worse last night," Richard said.

On a hunch, Thaddeus asked, "Is anyone's phone working?"

One by one, they checked their devices, switching them on. The screens remained dark.

"OK. Either we've been here longer than we think, and our phone batteries are all dead—which I find highly unlikely—or the electromagnetic field fried them."

"Wait—So, this device teleports arbitrary organic material to a random location?" Theo said. "What would be the point of that?"

"Maybe it's only arbitrary or random because we don't have all the facts yet," Thaddeus concluded. "What if it came back here because it is programmed to, or ..." He trailed off, eyes scanning the surrounding area. An orange flag stuck out of the sand about five feet from the hole where the device now sat. "Declan, do you remember what that marker was?"

"GPR picked up a weak signal under that spot," Declan said. "I think it was about five feet down, give or take. I guess when we found the artifact, we focused all our attention on that. We ne'er finished the rest of the search grid before those goons with the guns showed up."

Thaddeus turned to his son.

"We're not turning anything over to anyone until we have more answers. When was the last time you got your hands dirty?"

"Yeah, there's a reason I chose physics," Theo beamed with a slight grin. "Complex equations and theories don't ruin your clothes—or your washing machine."

***

Much of their camp had been ransacked, probably by the two men Declan humiliated just a day before. They had thrown bedding from tents and unceremoniously bashed the camp stove over a nearby rock.

"Someone has some serious anger issues," Theo said, surveying the mess.

"Score!" Richard called out. He stepped from behind the storage tent, grinning with a shovel held high above his head.

"Alright, Richie!" said Declan. "Let's get to work."

Thaddeus and Susie had hiked to the main road in hopes of flagging down an out-of-state tourist or vacationing family willing to give them a ride to town. It was a calculated risk, but it was also unlikely anyone would be looking for them this far from Denver.

The three men took turns digging and shuttling soil away in buckets. It was hot, thirsty work, but they had little choice. If something else buried here would shed light on the strange device, they needed to find it before anyone else did. After about an hour of work, the tip of Theo's shovel struck something solid. He bent down to brush the dirt away, expecting to find a boulder or a layer of sandstone. Instead, a gray, metallic edge protruded from beneath his feet.

"Guys," he yelled out, "I think I found what we're looking for."

Richard and Declan stood to either side and peered into the hole.

"Congratulations, Theo," Richard said. "You're now officially an archaeologist."

***

Chapter 6

The Jeep was still where they had left it. Declan's hunch about the limited traffic in the back alley had been correct. Thaddeus and Susie quickly cleared away the stacked crates and pallets and then made a beeline for the convenience store at the north end of town. The sheriff had called off the Amber Alert—but they still didn't need any unwanted attention from the sheriff or his deputies.

They topped off the tank at the *Express 24*, loaded up on water and snacks, and set out westward toward the rest of their group. Susie drove the back roads toward Dead Horse Point, then turned onto an old dirt Jeep trail that entered Canyonlands from the north. They didn't want to risk passing through the ranger station at the main gate.

After several rough miles, the trail joined the paved road, and they made good time reaching the turnoff toward their dig site.

Declan walked over as Susie pulled the battered old Jeep to a stop.

"It's just as you suspected, Professor," he said. "We found another device. It's smaller than the first one, but it appears it's made of the same stuff."

Richard and Theo were sitting under the dining fly, trying to stay out of the late morning sun. Susie brought them each a bottle of water, and they drank them down greedily. Declan took two from the back of the Jeep and drank the first in one go. He walked with Thaddeus toward the table where the new device lay.

The new object was about two feet by one foot. There was no clear way to determine its orientation. The item was flat for the most part; its upper surface stood just four or five inches above the tabletop. Two thin, flat flange-like shapes overlapped to form a type of cross fastened to the underside, and it appeared as though it was once part of something much more significant. A highly polished, mirror-like metallic dome took up almost half of the face of the object. It reflected the sun sharply from its silver-white surface. The remainder of the device was the same flat matte gray as the dodecahedron, with seventeen gold-colored shapes clustered across it in groups of various sizes. These resembled buttons, and the larger ones contained unrecognizable raised symbols.

Thaddeus looked the device over for a while, trying to determine its possible function or purpose. He had a hunch there was a connection between the two devices, a link that had somehow brought the larger device and everything around it back here.

After retrieving this new artifact, Theo, Declan, and Richard had hauled the original device back up to their camp. Declan and Richard placed it cautiously into the back of the Jeep. Susie covered it with two sleeping bags, leaving space on one side for the other device. Thaddeus and his son puzzled over the newest find.

"Were you able to get through to my father?" Richard asked.

"Eventually," said Thaddeus.

They had called a neighbor with a concocted story about an emergency at SPARC's research facility—the company owned by Richard's father. They told the older woman that they could not get through on the phone and would she please go next door and ask Mr. Hayes to take the call on her phone. After some lengthy discussion, she convinced him to come to the phone. Thaddeus explained their predicament and the need for the ruse. Gerald Hayes was incensed at the idea that the government would tap his phone and quite reluctant to get involved initially, but he ultimately agreed to meet them at his testing site outside Las Vegas.

***

Abraham Jensen had dreamed of a career in law enforcement for most of his life. His father had served in the military, and his grandfather was a small-town sheriff. Abe grew up idolizing both men. Unfortunately, he was rail-thin, asthmatic, and not particularly coordinated. He was unable to meet the physical requirements for the police academy.

Abe's true aptitude lay in computers—specifically programming, coding, and designing software. At twelve, he built his own PC from parts; by fourteen, he had written and sold several popular apps.

Throughout high school and college, he embraced new technology. In addition to taking numerous IT classes, other students sought him out for help with their projects. Abe relished the chance to solve a puzzle, to push the envelope of what software could accomplish.

After the police academy rejected him, he applied to the NSA's cyber-security division, where he quickly gained a reputation for both his technical skills and work ethic.

He'd headed up a couple of high-profile projects in DC and received approval to transfer to the new data facility in Utah. Now he was close to his family and working in a fascinating and rewarding field—even if his current bosses didn't recognize his true genius. Abe's dream now was to prove himself and someday run this facility.

Walking back from his lunch break, Abe grumbled—to no one in particular—about the miserable weekend shift. In his third full week at the facility, his lack of seniority had him working irregular hours despite his talents. He returned to his IT workstation to find an alert window flashing on his monitor.

After scanning thousands of images per second from cameras all over the country, facial recognition software had positively identified a person of interest—a high-priority target. Following protocol, Abe reviewed the feed and captured a segment of the video file, along with several still images that showed a full view of the subject's face. He pulled up the contact info of the operative working the case and forwarded the packet electronically via an encrypted connection. After confirming the packet uploaded correctly, he moved on to his other assigned tasks without another thought.

Twenty minutes later, Abe found himself in a small interrogation room face to face with Arthur Tomlinson himself. His large frame and broad shoulders were imposing. As the head of a secretive NSA Cybertech sub-division tied to the Defense Department, Tomlinson was well known around the facility—even if very few knew what he and his group actually did. There were rumors that he'd been in the CIA or perhaps military intelligence. Abe had a level-three security clearance; Black Eagle operatives, such as Tomlinson and his elite team, were several levels above that. Tomlinson had coined the unofficial Black Eagle nickname almost as a joke—a tongue-in-cheek reference to the Yankee White clearance required to work directly with the president.

Tomlinson was well-groomed and well dressed. His short dark hair always looked as though he'd just had it cut. Abe thought briefly that the man's suit likely cost more than Abe made in a month; the watch on his wrist then represented a year's salary. He wondered how Tomlinson could afford such items on a government salary but decided he probably didn't want to know. Some things were above your pay grade for a reason.

"Mr. Jensen, I've been looking over the packet you prepared for my team," Tomlinson said after several minutes.

He leaned back in his seat with his fingers interlaced across his chest. His body language was casual and relaxed, yet his steel-gray eyes bore into Abe's soul. It was all he could do to resist the urge to squirm in his seat.

"What is your clearance level?" Tomlinson asked, though he already knew the answer.

"T-3R, sir," Abe replied. "I've been with the NSA for two years and here in Bluffdale for three weeks."

"Son, I didn't ask for your life story," Tomlinson said. "I'm trying to determine if I need to increase your clearance or lock your ass up."

"I—I don't understand," Abe stammered.

Tomlinson opened the laptop sitting between them on the table. It was unmarked and was thinner and smaller than any laptop Abe had seen before. Tomlinson tapped a few keys and turned the screen toward him, and Abe saw one of the still images from the file he'd prepared.

"This is the file you sent, correct?"

Abe nodded. "Yes. Yes, sir."

"This time and date stamp in the corner—do you put that in, or is it from the camera? Does it come from the data source?"

He pointed to the bottom of the screen. It read 05/20/2023 - 08:43MDT.

Abe thought briefly about the irony; those in charge rarely have a clue about how things under their direction really work. He also thought if he played his cards right, this could become an opportunity to showcase his actual talents. Maybe one day, he'd be the guy with the thousand-dollar suits.

"The image is a live capture," Abe said. "Our software automatically logs the date and time and digitizes it for retrieval or analysis."

"And can it be altered or manipulated after the fact?"

"No, sir. The real-time encryption maintains the file integrity."

Tomlinson seemed to think about that for a long time. He locked his eyes on Abe as he said, "Alright, Mr. Jensen—Abraham—congratulations. You just jumped to T-5 clearance. I'll need you to work closely with my agents, Travers and Bronsky. We'll have some papers for you to sign, and you aren't to leave the facility until we finalize your clearance, understood?"

Abe nodded. His mouth was too dry to speak.

"I don't need to tell you that what I'm about to share with you cannot leave this room. You are not to discuss any details with anyone not directly assigned to this case." Tomlinson tapped a few more keys, and the screen showed two still images side by side. On the left was the still image Abe had included in his file; on the right, the same man entering a modern-looking building. The second image appeared to be a night photo. The man and those with him were awash in artificial light; the background faded to darkness a few dozen feet away.

"This image," Tomlinson said, "is from UC Denver just before one this morning."

Abe knew the first image was captured just a few hours ago from a security camera at a gas station outside Moab, Utah. He quickly did some math in his head.

"That's over two hundred miles from the first image," Abe said, frowning. "I suppose...if he drove straight through with minimal stops, it's possible."

"Closer to two-fifty. We don't believe he drove at all—his van is still at UC Denver. According to the cameras there, he never left."

***

Chapter 7

Liu Wei grew tired of waiting. His orders were clear; he was to locate and secure the artifact at all costs. His fellow operative had failed to report in and might be dead for all he knew. It would be a setback, but Chun Liu Wei had survived others before. Based on the continued activity at the university, the Americans had also failed to locate the object.

However unlikely, it seemed that a small group of geologists had somehow thwarted the NSA. Liu Wei didn't believe that would be the case for long. At least there was time. He could still complete his mission. With no contact from Nuan Lam, he needed to find another source of current intel.

He'd followed the two NSA agents from the university to the home of Thelonious Sterling, a physics professor. He watched from a distance as the dark-haired, larger man had scaled the short fence and entered the house. When he came out the back way ten minutes later, Liu Wei followed them to the FBI building downtown. Finally, they ended up at the Quality Inn.

He watched from outside until they entered room 213. Then he pulled into a parking space, lit a cigarette, and waited.

After thirty minutes, the two men climbed into their rented green Camry and drove off. Liu Wei waited ten more minutes to ensure they were well and truly gone before stepping out of his vehicle. He quickly donned a pair of coveralls with *MAINTENANCE* stenciled across the back. He pulled a red metal toolbox from the rear seat and confidently strode toward the motel. He climbed the stairs with purpose. When he reached unit 213, he picked the lock with deft skill and let himself inside.

***

The old Jeep pulled up to the main gate outside the SPARC facility, and the guard waved them through. True to his word, Richard's father had called ahead to arrange access. Theo pulled to a stop near the front of the building emblazoned with four-foot-high letters reading "Sustainable Power Alternatives Research Corporation." Gerald Hayes had founded SPARC in the early 2000s. He dumped every penny he had into the company to capitalize on the renewed interest in wind, solar, and other more sustainable energy sources. Solar power, in particular, was quite promising given Las Vegas's location. SPARC operated one of the largest concentrated solar power generators in the US. The investment had paid off—and Gerald Hayes was now one of the wealthiest men in Nevada.

Thaddeus had expected Richard's father to greet them when they arrived. Richard was pretty sure he wouldn't. His father had always been outwardly gregarious and social—if it meant winning over investors or sealing a lucrative business deal. If you didn't have anything of value—anything Gerald Hayes valued—you'd be lucky to get the time of day out of him.

A rather pretty woman in her early thirties approached them as they entered the lobby of the building. Her auburn hair was swept back in a ponytail and held tight by an abalone clip. Beneath her pristine lab coat, she wore a thin turquoise turtleneck and a navy skirt. To Susie, her outfit seemed odd—given the desert heat—until she felt the chill herself. Like many desert dwellers, Las Vegas, Phoenix, and Tucson inhabitants often kept the indoor air colder than necessary.

"Welcome to SPARC," she said. Her voice was pleasant enough, though the accent belonged in the Midwest rather than the middle of the Mojave Desert.

"Mr. Hayes sends his apologies," she continued. "He wanted to greet you himself, but he had a prior commitment he could not reschedule. He asked me to meet you in his place."

Richard wasn't sure if he was more upset or relieved. He hadn't seen his father in almost a year. He had spent his early childhood desperate for his father's acceptance and attention. He had given up on acceptance by the time he reached his teens and was content to spend the old man's money. Richard barely made it through high school and flunked out of both USC's and UNLV's business programs.

They'd finally reached a tenable truce. Richard agreed to apply himself and earn his business degree *if* he could study in Salt Lake City at the University of Utah. There he could also pursue his interest in geoscience. Getting out of Gerald's shadow had actually been good for Richard. Now, back in Nevada, he began to experience the same sense of dread he always got around his father.

"I'm Doctor Lisa Kowalski." She reached out to shake Thaddeus's hand. "Doctor Sterling, I presume?" Her smile was genuine and warm.

Theo stepped in front of his father in one smooth motion and shook her hand.

"That's me," he said, grinning from ear to ear. "It's nice to meet you, Doctor Kowalski. Allow me to introduce my traveling companions." He turned and gestured at each in turn. "Declan Cole, Susie Yang, Richard Hayes, and my father—Doctor Sterling."

Her cheeks flushed slightly, and she looked momentarily puzzled.

"Ignore my son, Doctor," Thaddeus said apologetically. "He's always been a joker. It seems we have a few doctors in our group. Perhaps you could just call me Thaddeus."

"Certainly, Doc—Thaddeus. And you can call me Lisa." Turning to the others, she focused on Richard. "How have you been, Richard?"

He shrugged, an awkward and pained expression on his face.

***

Men in lab coats carefully unloaded the two unusual objects from the back of the Jeep. They cradled the larger device in a secure harness suspended from what looked to Declan like a cherry picker hoist used to lift engine blocks. The smaller unit was secured with nylon straps to a heavy cart with pneumatic wheels. Rather than rolling them to the main building, with its adobe-colored brick and thick green glass, they moved the objects toward an outbuilding resembling a small airplane hangar.

One of the men scanned an access badge, entering the code that triggered a roll-up door. Theo watched as light spilled out across the paved area surrounding the building. The sun had set unnoticed—the few thin clouds briefly trapped the last red and purple rays before relenting and giving way to the darkness. One by one, the stars appeared overhead. A few at first, then clusters of them shone down on the small facility.

Other than a few exterior lights in the parking area, the inky blackness of night consumed the desert around them. To the east, Theo could see the lights of Las Vegas, though they were several miles away. Countless megawatts of halogen and neon lights cut through the night, obliterating the stars like a human-made sunrise.

The Luxor pyramid's beacon stood out like a blue-white dagger thrust into the heart of the city.

"It's beautiful, isn't it?" Theo was startled by Susie's voice—unaware that she was standing next to him. He didn't know how long he had stood transfixed, staring up at the vast space above them.

"It's funny," she said. "From this distance, it reminds me of home. Growing up in Guangzhou, I never saw the stars between the light pollution—and the actual pollution. My first time really seeing a night sky was when I was on a youth field trip when I was thirteen. I spent hours staring at the Milky Way after the other girls had gone to bed. When we went home, I remember looking out the bus window as we approached the city. It looked a lot like that."

They stood in shared silence a moment longer before Thaddeus beckoned them inside.

Though it was late evening, the hangar/laboratory facility was bustling with efficient activity. Several men and women in lab coats—some taking copious notes on tablets—focused on half a dozen small projects at worktables along the far wall. Near the center of the space, a vast column of bright, tightly woven copper mesh stretched from floor to ceiling. Heavy cables ran from the top and bottom of the metal structure to insulators and what looked like electrical transformers. No one even looked up as the technicians wheeled the strange device toward the most massive Faraday cage Theo had ever seen.

***

Tomlinson's call caught Travers and Bronsky in the middle of an early lunch at the *Starlite Diner.* The food there wasn't so much good as it was convenient. Their motel was a mere two blocks away. Nate dropped a twenty-dollar bill and a handful of loose change on the table and took the uneaten half of Bronsky's ham and swiss, and they both bolted toward the door.

The military had conditioned them to travel light, and their current assignment was no different. The agents packed their modest bags quickly and made the short drive to Denver International in relative silence. Steve was secretly glad to finally be rid of the puke-green Camry as they dropped it off at the rental area and took the shuttle to the charter terminal. A sleek black Gulfstream jet was already warming up its engines when they arrived. The pilot stowed their bags as the two men found their seats for the two-hour flight to Las Vegas.

***

Chapter 8

As technicians strapped the larger device to a cradle-like table, others poked and prodded at the smaller device, trying to glean clues from its design or markings. They carefully removed the flat plates attached to the back of the device, exposing a thin seam around the outer casing. They slowly separated the upper portion from the back panel, taking care not to disconnect or damage the transparent, hair-like fibers that ran throughout the object. Doctor Kowalski had excused herself to oversee the procedure.

The level of activity in the small space was ramping up, with everyone laser-focused on their immediate task. Thaddeus and his associates had been all but forgotten. They stood huddled together just inside the hangar door and tried not to get run over in the excitement.

Declan heard the lock in the door behind them disengage. An older man with thinning hair and thick eyeglasses pulled it partway open. He wore a lab coat like everyone else, but beneath it was a pale blue Oxford shirt and a thin black tie. He was speaking to someone else Declan couldn't see, and with all the noise happening within the ample space, it was difficult to make out precisely what the man was saying. Nevertheless, the older man was apparently conducting an animated discussion with someone standing just outside, based on his voice and body language. Then Declan saw the Bluetooth device in the man's left ear and realized he was likely on a phone call.

Finally, the man turned his attention toward them and stepped fully into the room, allowing the door to close behind him. He strode forward and extended his hand to Thaddeus with a grin.

"Doctor Thaddeus Sterling," he said. "I'm glad I finally get to meet you in person. Richard has spoken repeatedly about the positive influence you've had on him."

Thaddeus shook the man's hand and returned the smile.

"Mister Hayes," he said, "I have to admit I'm more than a little impressed with your setup here."

He introduced Gerald Hayes to Theo and the rest of the group—though he didn't have to introduce Richard.

"Richard," Gerald said. "It sounds like you've had an eventful couple of days."

His mannerism—warm and inviting when speaking with Thaddeus just moments before—instantly became stiff and emotionless. Richard's companions noticed this, and an awkward silence passed between them all before Richard finally spoke, his voice strained.

"You could say that. Thanks for helping us out, sir. I know you're busy these days."

"To be honest, I'm quite busy most days," Gerald said, turning his attention back to the group. "We just signed several very lucrative contracts and are under a tight deadline to deliver the technology on time and on budget. That's the main reason so many of my people are working late—and on the weekend besides."

Throughout Richard's entire life, his father had been a workaholic. He preferred immersing himself in work to spending any quality time with his family. Richard's mother was the one who encouraged him, attended his little league games, and consoled him when he was bullied at school. Gerald was entertaining potential investors in Dubai when his wife was diagnosed with advanced pancreatic cancer. He was away in Europe when she passed away—leaving Richard and his younger sister, Cara, emotionally adrift.

A loud rumbling arose from the rear of the hangar building as a thick, segmented wall of metal plates moved along tracks set in the floor and ceiling. Several technicians hurried to get out of the way, leaving just Lisa inside as the metal wall bisected the building.

"What's happening?" Susie asked.

Gerald waved a dismissive hand without looking in her direction.

"We have a series of scans and tests lined up based on your earlier experience. Don't worry. The Faraday cage will inhibit a runaway energy ramp-up. We've been doing this type of thing for twenty years, and we are taking every precaution."

He raised a finger and turned away, touching his earpiece. He quickly stepped back toward the exterior door and unlocked it, pushing it open.

"Ah, gentlemen," he said. "Perfect timing. We were just about to begin."

"Oh, bollocks." Declan's face paled, and he took a half-step back as Mr. Ray-Ban and Mr. Wraparound strode through the door.

Richard spun on his father, rage in his voice. "You sold us out, you heartless son of a bitch!"

***

Leaning in, Lisa pressed the probe's tip into a slight depression on one facet of the matte-gray object. She keyed a command into the terminal on the mobile workstation to her left. A loud, low hum filled the air as the EMF gauge topped 55,000 mT (miliTesla) before displaying an error, represented by a series of *E*s. She frowned and checked the reading a second time. Lisa reset the meter and then moved to the next facet.

The air-conditioning and significant overhead circulating fans did little to slow her perspiration, which she could feel beading on her forehead and trickling between her shoulder blades. A thick, sheathed cable tethered her to the Faraday cage and grounded her against any possible electrical or magnetic danger. Still, she felt a growing unease, as though trapped with this strange object in some mismatched technological Thunderdome.

Silhouetted figures watched her from behind inch-thick glass in the surrounding partition as she moved the EMF generator to one side of the workspace. She selected another unit that slightly resembled a dentist's X-ray. The device had a focused lens on one end—the other end attached to a segmented arm allowing a complete range of motion. Angling the lens to within a few inches of the nearest surface depression, she slipped on a pair of amber-lensed glasses and toggled the power.

A hum filled the room, growing louder and deeper as seconds passed. Lisa watched her readouts closely as she felt the hairs on her neck beginning to stand on end. The facets around the object began to glow a deep, almost imperceptible purple. The hum deepened, and she could feel the vibration in her bones. She switched off the powerful laser and swung the arm away from the device. The vibrations continued. The numbers on the display screen nearest her climbed incrementally until they read 5,300 MW. After a full five minutes, the hum began to subside, and the power levels quickly dropped away to almost nothing. Lisa breathed a sigh of relief as she disengaged her tether and stepped from the cage.

"That's *it*?" Steve Bronsky said, a note of incredulity in his voice.

"*That*," Gerald said, "was more than double the electricity the Hoover Dam generates daily. This could be a gamechanger if we can find the right frequency to sustain the output."

***

Liu Wei touched down just before sunset. A Chinese aviation and logistics firm owned the private jet, and Liu Wei's people had quickly arranged the flight. Corporate executives often traveled to Las Vegas—both for business and pleasure. He wore an expensive suit, and no one had paid him any notice as he disembarked from the plane at McCarran International Airport.

Liu Wei gathered his bags and made his way to the waiting car, issuing a curt greeting to the three other agents inside. He produced a small device from a pocket and switched it on. Immediately, a directional arrow overlaid a road map of the surrounding area.

The tracking device he'd placed in the luggage of the NSA agents appeared as a bright red dot some twenty miles to the west.

Chapter 9

"Wow, you *do* look like shit," Tomlinson said as he met Travers and Bronsky in the hallway of the SPARC main building. A pair of NSA agents watched over the hangar, and Abe Jensen worked with Hayes's staff, dissecting what they were calling the control module. Tomlinson had also replaced the regular gate guards with a second Black Eagle team. The entire SPARC facility was on total lockdown.

"Yeah, well, you should see the other guy," Steve said, a sheepish grin on his face.

Tomlinson looked through the window into the conference room where the small group of geologists waited to be debriefed, then back at Bronsky.

"Uh-huh," he said. "Why don't you two get cleaned up and grab some shuteye. Meet up back here in, say, six hours?"

"Sure, sir. Thanks," said Nate. The two men turned and left as Tomlinson entered the small boardroom.

"Are we being arrested?" It was the older man, Sterling.

"Not exactly," said Tomlinson. "Unfortunately, you folks have stumbled into something that could directly affect national security. Until we know more about what we're dealing with, I can't allow anyone to leave. Also, it appears that several of you assaulted a pair of federal agents." He spoke to the group, but his eyes were firmly on Declan. "But we'll overlook that if you're willing to cooperate."

He casually took a seat at the head of the small table. He pulled a small pad from his jacket and began to make notes.

"First off, I need to know who else you've told about the device."

***

Nate nodded to the Asian guard standing at the gate as they drove by the security booth. The other man sitting inside pressed the button that raised the bar without looking up from his desk. Nate thought he sensed something odd but chalked it up to exhaustion. He and Steve hadn't slept in nearly twenty hours. He drove off, never seeing the men concealed behind the guard shack—or the two dead NSA agents.

Once the SUV was out of sight, two MSS operatives joined Liu Wei and moved toward the oversized hangar. The third remained at the gate. The three agents, dressed all in black, moved silently through the shadows sizing up their target. They needed to act before anyone tried to contact the guards and before daylight stole their meager cover.

***

Lisa quickly scanned the readouts as the low, almost inaudible vibration increased. The sound waves progressed from the infrasonic spectrum to a deep hum she could feel in her chest. Rising further, it became a buzzing in her ears, and various items throughout the lab space began to vibrate and rattle. The waves shortened, and the volume increased exponentially.

The output gauges surpassed the previous reading, and ultraviolet halos formed around the indentations on the object's surface. The reaction began much sooner than it did in their first experiment and faster than when they repeated it thirty minutes later—only she hadn't initiated the buildup. The device had begun cycling up on its own.

Tiny sparks crackled across the pentagonal plates of the device, and Lisa began to smell ozone. The power output had redlined on the gauges for the transformers, and for a moment, she thought they might overload—a virtual impossibility given all their safety protocols. She had her hand on the phone to call Mr. Hayes, but the object held her transfixed.

The air around the shape began to shimmer. Lisa briefly thought she saw the device become translucent as a bright bluish glow surrounded it. The moment passed, and the output dropped off rapidly.

She moved to check the display nearest the Faraday cage when an ear-splitting *bang!* and a blinding flash of light threw her from her feet. Blackness engulfed the entire hangar—the flash blindness hung like an artificial red sun in the center of her field of vision. She tried to rise, but her arms felt like lead. Her eyelids drooped, and she slumped back to the floor.

***

Nate had been troubled by something he couldn't quite grasp since they'd pulled away from the SPARC facility. He thrust his elbow sharply into Steve's ribs. He'd been snoring for the last ten miles.

"What the hell?!" Steve sputtered, cracking one eye and scowling at Nate.

"I need you to check something for me, will you?" Nate said without taking his eyes from the road. "See if you can pull up the names of the agents Tomlinson put on the gate."

Steve grumbled something unintelligible but produced a small tablet and began entering commands. It took several minutes, but he was finally able to pull up the data.

"First guy's name is Milo Henreid. Former Seal outta Wisconsin," Steve said. "Ugly bald guy—six foot two."

The description matched the guard Nate had seen in the shack, though the man hadn't actually looked up. He hadn't actually looked awake, which was part of what had been nagging at Nate.

"What about the second guy?" Nate said.

"Rob Jackson," Steve said. "He's—"

Nate hit the gas and swerved across two lanes simultaneously. Steve braced himself as the SUV exited the highway, still traveling over seventy. Nate braked hard, turned left at the bottom of the exit, and headed for the westbound onramp, pushing the engine to its limit.

Rob "Action" Jackson was a former all-state linebacker from Alabama. Nate had met him in Afghanistan before an IED had sent him home. Rob Jackson was six foot seven and probably weighed two-hundred and twenty pounds. He was also African American.

Steve looked at Nate, puzzled, and then at the highway speeding beneath them. Nate pressed the autodial on the steering wheel for Tomlinson's number, but his call went directly to voicemail.

"Damnit!" he said, pushing the vehicle to nearly one hundred miles per hour.

***

The conference room plunged into darkness, followed a second later by a distant *pop!* like a firework—or a gunshot. Tomlinson rose immediately as if by instinct and moved to the door.

"Stay here, all of you," he said. "It could be nothing, but I don't need you getting underfoot nonetheless."

He produced a penlight and used its light to move toward the open stairway down to the main lobby. In the dead silence, they heard his footsteps fade as he left the building.

"Like hell I will," Declan said.

"Whatever's happenin', I'm not hangin' around here. Who's with me?"

No one spoke up right away. Then Thaddeus spoke in low, even tones. "Declan, we're already in enough hot water. Please, just sit back down, and—"

"He's right," Richard said. "Doctor Sterling, we can't just sit here. They're going to take our discovery away from us—possibly the greatest find in the past hundred years—and either bury it away or let my dad use it to make himself even richer." Though they couldn't see his face, the anger and hurt were evident.

"I'm in, too," Theo said.

"Fine," said Thaddeus with a sigh.

"Who knows—maybe prison's underrated."

One by one, the group filed out. Without the convenience of a light source, they had to feel their way along the hall toward the stairs.

When they had gone, Susie felt around the table for the phones Tomlinson had taken from them. When she located her device, she removed the specially shielded back and flipped a hidden switch. The screen came to life with a soft blue glow. She quickly pressed a preset series of keys and slipped it into her pocket. Silently she turned right at the doorway and made her way to the rear fire stairs.

***

Liu Wei felt the vibration in his jacket and pulled out his phone as the other two Chinese agents wrestled the device into the secured chest bolted in the cargo area of the SUV. He glanced up and saw the first pink tendrils of light painting the few thin clouds overhead as the coming dawn stole across the desert to the east.

"You! Stop whatever you're doing there."

Liu Wei drew his pistol, turned, and fired in one cat-like motion. In the dim light, he watched the red blotch blossom on the man's chest, spreading quickly across the front of his blue Oxford shirt. Eyes bulged behind thick-lensed glasses, and disbelief twisted the man's face as he stumbled before dropping to his back.

Without another thought, Liu Wei turned back to the other agents.

"Gǎnkuài! Tāmen jiāng suíshí zài zhèlǐ!" he said, gesturing for them to move faster.

Lam better hurry or she will miss her ride, he thought.

***

Arthur Tomlinson had seen combat. He had been under fire on numerous occasions and had enjoyed a long government career for two reasons. His instincts under duress surpassed those of his contemporaries, and he knew better than to stick his neck out without plenty of good intel. When he heard the silenced shot and saw Hayes's body in the parking lot, adrenaline almost got the better of him. He drew his weapon and waited behind cover to assess the threat he was facing. He caught sight of movement to his right and drew down before realizing it was Yang, the female geologist. She was running from the rear of the main building—right into whoever had just shot Hayes.

"Yang, get down!" he shouted. He raised from his crouch enough for her to see him and tried to gesture her over. She glanced back briefly but only increased her pace. There was another silenced gunshot, and Tomlinson felt a sharp pain in his right shoulder.

He dropped his gun and grabbed at the wound.

The black SUV roared to life, kicking up a rooster tail of dust as it sped toward the gate. Tomlinson fired several shots toward the fleeing vehicle with his gun in his left hand. He knew he had little hope of hitting it but hoped the noise would warn the men at the guard shack. He watched, his mouth agape, as one of the guards *climbed into* the SUV as it slowed at the open gate. It drove to the end of the access road and accelerated west onto the highway.

***

Chapter 10

Tomlinson sat in the hangar lab surveying the aftermath and taking a mental tally of what the previous night had cost them. The thick metal door hung askew on its hinges, the frame torn and twisted inward where the locking mechanism had been. An eight-foot section cut from the side of the Faraday cage lay crumpled and bent on the floor. Many damaged chairs and small electronics were strewn throughout the space.

Henreid and Jackson—veterans and two of his best Black Eagles—lay dead at the facility's main gate. On loan from NSA's Vegas team, Victor Thomas had taken a bullet to the back of the head as he patrolled outside the lab building.

His partner, Jim Lewis, had been lucky; he was inside the building when the Chinese agents blew the door and tossed in a powerful flash grenade paired with a fast-acting tranquilizing gas. Tomlinson knew from past dealings with the Ministry of State Security agents it might just as well have been a nerve agent.

Gerald Hayes had a bullet in his lung, lost a lot of blood, and probably wasn't going to pull through. Tomlinson had personally put him and his son on an NSA chopper to Mountain View Hospital, but the EMTs weren't optimistic about his chances.

Add to all that the loss of the artifact from Utah. Somewhere out in the darkness, Chinese agents were speeding away with possibly the most world-changing discovery in fifty years.

Yang Shu was working with the Chinese agents; God knows how much intel she'd shared (and may still be sharing) with them. NSA data teams were combing through her history, determining if Chinese agents recruited her at the university or if she was another sleeper agent.

For years, the FBI and HSI had investigated the flow of cutting-edge research from US universities that somehow made its way to China. These instances had increased, and several students, researchers, and faculty had been arrested and convicted of spying for China. As foreign technology and medical researchers faced harsher scrutiny, China began placing spies in lower-visibility disciplines such as geology.

Travers and Bronsky finished interviewing the scientists from the lab and walked over to where Tomlinson sat. His face was ashen and drawn, and he had a bandage wrapped around his right shoulder. He stared through the damaged doorway into the parking lot beyond, absent-mindedly turning his ruined cellphone over in his left hand.

"Sir, are you sure you're alright?" Nate asked.

"Yeah, you don't look so good," Steve added.

Tomlinson turned to look at the two men and fixed his gaze on Bronsky.

"Look who's talking," he said. He held up his phone. One corner had been destroyed, and both the case and screen were shattered. "So much for my indestructible case. I think I'm gonna rescind my five-star review. Probably saved my life, though, so ..."

The bullet had struck the phone in his jacket pocket and shattered, sending shrapnel into his upper arm. If not for the phone, the medics had said he probably would be keeping Hayes company on his flight, or worse.

***

Abe stood over the workbench, looking over the tangle of nearly invisible thin fibers strung beneath the control box. On closer examination, these appeared to be a type of fiber-optic cables, which made sense given everything he'd been briefed on so far regarding the two strange devices. Concentrated laser light had activated the larger device, somehow teleporting five people to a different state. It was reasonable to assume that light was the power source for this object also. He closed his eyes and tried to visualize the various pathways of the cables.

"How are you coming with your research?"

Abe's eyes snapped open, and he turned to see the man standing next to him, looking over the device.

"Slow," he said. "I've always considered myself pretty good with puzzles, but I usually have at least an idea of what the end result is supposed to look like or do. This"—he gestured at the jumble on the table—"I don't even know what it's supposed to do, or even if it's all here."

"I'm no good with tech," the man said, "but I think I'm pretty good with theory. Maybe we can collaborate and figure it out together."

Abe put out his hand. "Abe Jensen."

"Theo Sterling. Good to meet you."

***

"Doctor Kowalski, the clock is ticking," Tomlinson said. "I need every available resource you have working on the remaining piece of tech. If it truly is linked to the missing device, it may be our only path toward its recovery."

Lisa stood stoically and looked the man in the eye. She wanted to rail at him about the tragedy the device had already caused. Her boss (and mentor) was fighting for his life, and her lab was in shambles. Then her demeanor softened as she thought of the people he, too, had just lost.

"Alright," she said finally. "We'll do our best."

"Thank you," he said. Then he turned to the two agents that arrived at Hayes's request the previous evening. "Take Sterling and the Irishman and head west on the interstate. I have a hunch they'll try to load the device onto a cargo ship at the Port of Los Angeles. They'll likely try to take advantage of the fact that it's the busiest shipping port on the West Coast. Customs and HSI are already on alert, but they can't check twenty-five thousand containers a day. Something's bound to slip through. Either catch up to them or drive them further west. We'll keep trying everything we can from here."

Travers and Bronsky looked at each other, then at Tomlinson. Bronsky's face had darkened, and his jaw was set, but he said nothing. He knew better than to question his boss.

"Sir?" Nate spoke up for them both.

"Begging your pardon, but they're *geologists*, for hell's sake. Why take them along?"

Tomlinson stood to his full height and pointed toward the back of the lab where Thaddeus and Declan sat, his face hard.

"These two *geologists* are the only ones who've seen the device operate—really operate. I don't mean some glorified battery experiment, either. Imagine if the Chinese get that thing back to Beijing and reverse engineer it. Now imagine armed Chinese troops suddenly materializing inside the White House, or the Capital, or hell, anywhere."

"Yes, sir," Nate said.

His face paled a bit as Tomlinson's suggestion hit home. When Hayes had called the device a game-changer, none of them considered the implications and possible danger it could pose in the wrong hands.

The two men excused themselves and made their way toward the pair sitting along the far wall.

"Well, this will be awkward, to say the least," Steve said.

"Just keep it professional until *after* we get the device back," Nate said. "After that, I don't care what you do to the overgrown Leprechaun."

***

Theo traced cables with his hands as Abe sketched out a makeshift schematic on a tablet. Occasionally he would carefully lift a bundle out of the way with the tip of his stylus to get a better look at the workings underneath. They'd been at it for nearly an hour, but the inner workings of the device and the purpose of the various buttons still eluded them.

"What's the pattern?" Abe said, setting down his tablet and running a hand through his dark hair.

He'd repaired and even built complex computers before, but he always knew what each component did and how they interacted together. SAS, eSATA, and ATX cables each had a unique look, color, and connectors. This device used one uniform type of fiber optic cable and connector for everything. It felt like trying to assemble a jigsaw puzzle where all the pieces were blank. He had no idea what the big picture was supposed to be.

Doctor Kowalski wheeled a large cart alongside the table where the two men pored over the module.

"How's it coming?" she asked.

"The schematic is nearly complete," Theo said without looking up. "But it may as well be a flow chart where the lines connect only question marks."

He continued tracing the filament in his hand to where it attached beneath the large half-sphere.

"Abe, take a look at this," he said. There was a note of excitement in his voice.

Both Abe and Lisa crowded close to see what he was pointing out. Nearly every cable originated (or ended) behind the silver dome. They flowed from a circular grid of connectors to corresponding points behind every button on the object's face. They had seen no markings anywhere inside the device, and Abe had halfway joked that there should have been an owner's manual—or at the very least a *Quick Start* guide.

Theo's finger had come to rest on a small symbol etched just above the connection. It was so minuscule they'd completely overlooked it.

"This matches one of the symbols on the larger buttons," Abe said. Now he, too, sounded excited.

Theo made a mental note of the mark and carefully turned the cover over. The other end of the cable was attached to the button that bore the same symbol.

***

It was safe to assume the NSA expected Liu Wei to take the faster, more direct route to Los Angeles. There was no disguising his ultimate destination; instead, he would have to outthink his opponents. Be the cat instead of the mouse.

The Americans probably already had their satellites' cameras trained on the stretch of interstate freeway west of Las Vegas. It was likely that even now, several NSA agency vehicles were racing toward the city of Baker, hoping to intercept the Chinese agents and recover the device. His contact alerted him to this possibility and suggested an alternate path—taking them instead south onto US 95. It would add several hours and more than one hundred miles to their journey, but they stood a much better chance of reaching their rendezvous point undetected.

The black SUV left the highway just outside Needles, California, and pulled into an abandoned self-storage facility. Liu Wei drove through the unlocked gate toward the oversized door of a unit built for boat storage. Nuan Lam and the other three agents helped him unfasten the heavy vault containing the stolen object and transfer it to a waiting U-Haul trailer. An advance team had set this up the previous day per his instructions.

When the large door rolled open again, three older model pickups rolled out and onto the highway, each pulling a nondescript trailer. Nuan Lam rode with Liu Wei; the other agents would take slightly different routes. If somehow a satellite had picked them up (though Liu Wei thought it highly unlikely), they wouldn't know which vehicle had the device—becoming a high-stakes game of the bean and cups.

They were on schedule, and until now, everything had gone according to plan, yet Liu Wei felt uneasy. He couldn't shake a growing sense of dread that made his skin crawl.

***

Chapter 11

Nate drove the graphite-colored Rhino GX as the four men headed west along the highway toward California. Tomlinson had commandeered it from the Las Vegas office for its off-road capabilities, should they need them. Another NSA team followed a mile or so behind them. No one had said a word in the hour since leaving the SPARC facility—the only sound was the deep rumble of the diesel engine pushing them onward.

Steve sat to his right, scowling as if he'd just eaten a dead mouse and staring out the front windshield. Nate glanced briefly in the rearview and met the level gaze of both of his reluctant passengers. Finally, he couldn't stand the silence any longer.

"Look, I doubt we'll ever be BFFs, but we've got to put the whole misunderstanding in the desert behind us."

"You pointed a gun at me," Thaddeus said flatly.

"And me as well," said Declan. "You pistol-whipped poor Richie and cuffed him, too. Where I come from, that's a wee bit more than a bloody *misunderstanding*."

Steve whipped around in his seat and pointed to his ruined face.

"Well, from here, it looks like maybe we're even. The fact that I didn't drop you the minute we entered the SPARC lab—"

"That's enough!" Nate said, raising his voice. "Right now, Chinese agents are speeding away with a priceless piece of tech—one that they would never have gotten their hands on if you hadn't sucker-punched us and took off halfway across the western US. Yeah, I know we might have been heavy-handed with you. We were under specific orders, and I can't change what happened. But my boss is counting on the four of us to somehow pull a miracle out of our asses and prevent an international incident. The only way we're going to do that is if we work together."

He took a deep breath and let it out, trying to get his emotions in check. They drove on in silence once again.

***

Abe had expected to find something equivalent to a CPU, data drive, or motherboard—something that would give him some idea of how the device operated. Theo had located more connecting points with symbols matching the buttons on the device's face, but there were no other solid-state components other than the half-sphere. They had been combing over Abe's schematic when one of SPARC's engineers discovered something they had all missed. As they huddled around the device, talking over each other and trying to see the pattern, a small, quiet Japanese woman placed two fingers in her mouth and blew an ear-splitting whistle—cutting off the conversation like a knife. They all turned at once in her direction.

"It's not a computer," she said. "You're looking at this all wrong." She pointed to the drawing on Abe's tablet, turning it so they could all see. "There should be a power supply cable—something attached where all these other fibers originate, but not connected anywhere else on the device."

Armed with this new information, Abe soon spotted a connection shaped differently from the others near the center of the dome-shaped feature, buried in among the nest of optic cables. They had overlooked it because whatever should connect here had been stripped out.

They managed to disengage the connector by depressing three small pins at its base. Lisa had two of her people locate the correct thickness of fiber optic from their workshop, and they created a makeshift concentrator to attach to the argon laser.

Doctor Kowalski powered it on, then turned the dial slowly, increasing the output in minute increments. The last thing she wanted to do was overload the device or burn out some key element or worse.

Unlike the larger device, the unit didn't buzz or hum or make any sound. Lisa continued to increase the output from the laser, but they had no way to know if anything would happen.

After several minutes, she was about to give up and power off when a ring of blue light suddenly appeared surrounding the silver dome. Each of the symbols in the larger buttons glowed, backlit with the same deep blue light.

"Hot damn!" Abe said and pumped a fist in the air.

Lisa looked to Theo and then to Abe. She extended an index finger and pressed one of the buttons. Nothing happened. She pressed another with the same result.

On her fifth try, dozens of pinpoints of light shone from the dome, forming a holographic pattern roughly six inches from the surface.

"What is it?" Abe asked.

Theo leaned in for a better look.

"If I didn't know better, I'd say it was a starfield."

***

Nuan Lam grew more anxious with every mile. She hadn't anticipated the past few days' events—How could she? When the Ministry came to her family home, they spoke about duty, responsibility, and national security. She was only eighteen. What did she know about any of that?

Her father worked a menial factory job and barely made enough to pay their bills. Her mother had worked on an assembly line until an accident left her partially disabled. She lost the use of her right hand and now had to use a cane for support.

Her father urged her to accept the assignment the Ministry was offering her. She would get an education (one they could never afford), and the government would provide her parents with a stipend to help ease their financial burden.

Her mother would not go against her husband, but Lam could tell she was uncomfortable sending their daughter so far away.

Lam signed the papers, and the agency immediately sent her for in-depth training. The Ministry built her a new identity—Yang Shu. They issued identification in the new name, and she had, in essence, become Yang Shu from that day forward.

To fit in at the American university, she started going by Susie. For six years, she attended classes by day and ferried sensitive documents to dead-drop locations at night. It was a pure coincidence she had been part of Doctor Sterling's team in the Utah desert—a case of being in the right place at the right time.

Now she wasn't sure where the right place was. She was loyal to China and knew that her parents needed her to fulfill her duty. She knew that her people needed to keep up with the Americans if they wanted to continue to grow their economy. To refuse to do what they asked of her amounted to betraying her family and her country.

Yet deeper down, part of her felt that what she had been doing the past several years was wrong. She had gotten to know many of her classmates, and even developed close friendships. Essentially stealing their ideas—their hard work—felt like a betrayal of its own.

She saw Richard's unarmed father shot for merely being in the wrong place.

Lam quietly looked out the window, wrestling with her thoughts as Liu Wei drove on through Southern California. The engine drowned out the low hum coming from behind them. In the sunlight, she couldn't see the bright blue light from the trailer as it grew exponentially, then eventually faded away.

***

Richard and Cara sat in the back seat of the Town Car as the driver passed through the gate and pulled to a stop at the main entrance to their family estate. Richard hadn't been home in over a year. Now he was coming to grips with the fact that he and his sister were the only family they each had left.

The bullet had struck one of Gerald's ribs and shattered—sending metal shards slicing through his chest. It really was a wonder he hadn't bled out waiting for the helicopter that flew him and Richard to the Las Vegas hospital.

Cara had arrived while their father was in the operating room, and she and Richard took turns holding each other and pacing the waiting room floor. Finally, the surgeon joined them, his face exhausted and grim.

They had removed part of Gerald's right lung; the damage was too extensive to save it. He'd also needed several units of blood. They moved him to a private room in the ICU; Richard and Cara were welcome to sit with him, although he hadn't yet regained consciousness. The doctor said it would take several weeks, but he should make a full recovery.

After a while, Cara went to try to locate some food. Neither of them had eaten in hours. Richard sat in the chair near his father's bed and waited for her to return. He dozed off, only to be awakened by the alarms of his father's monitors. A nurse pushed him roughly out the door, and the crash team wheeled Gerald back down the hall into surgery.

One of the bullet fragments had nicked an artery, they said. The surgeons had missed it in the initial rush to save his life. By the time they got him back into the operating room, it was too late. He was gone.

***

Several miles outside of Palo Verde, two CHP motorcycle officers pulled over an older model pickup truck for expired tags on the trailer.

I-10 was one of several east-west freeways that provided a convenient conduit for drug traffic headed from Mexico, through Arizona, and on to LA. The Highway Patrol vigilantly watched for suspicious vehicles that might fit this profile and frequently stopped them hoping to stem the tide. Officers knew a broken taillight or expired tags could lead to a big bust.

The driver of the old Ford had been cooperative, calm, and even pleasant. The Asian man apologized for his oversight, claiming that he hadn't used the trailer in several months. His sister asked him to help her move on short notice, and he had neglected to check the tags before leaving home.

If the CHP officer had let them go with a warning—or even with a citation—the traffic stop would have been over in a matter of a few minutes. But when he asked the driver to open the trailer, his trained eye noticed a slight, almost imperceptible shift in the man's demeanor. The driver recovered quickly and asked his passenger to (slowly) open the glove box and retrieve the trailer key.

The two officers, hands resting on their service pistols, watched intently as the compartment opened. When they saw it was mostly empty, they relaxed just a bit.

They never saw the shots coming until it was too late.

One died instantly; the other lived long enough to call in the incident and give a vehicle description.

When the 10-00 call went out over the CHP radio, Ron DeSalvo was just a few miles from the town of Palo Verde. He hit his lights and siren and sped west.

***

Chapter 12

Tomlinson cashed in every favor he had, and when that didn't work, he resorted to threats. Two entire teams of NSA tech specialists were combing through satellite imagery to pin down the truck's location and trace the feeds back to where it originated. Somewhere after they left Las Vegas, the Chinese agents had switched vehicles. He needed to know when and how they did this and—more importantly—whether he had to track down more than just the single pickup.

Using the known location of the CHP shooting as a starting point, they identified the model, year, and make of the truck. The gray trailer was an older U-Haul and probably stolen and repainted. Rewinding the feed, the team back-traced its route along I-10 to US95, then north—until a large band of clouds obstructed their view. They continued to sweep the highway, running the images backward. They picked up the truck again briefly just south of Needles.

After what felt like hours, they pinpointed the storage facility. They now knew they were tracking not one but three possible targets. A hastily assembled NSA/HSI team was en route to the facility to ensure the device wasn't still there. Looking at the shattered phone before him, Tomlinson knew he'd probably used up his supply of luck for the foreseeable future. He slid the desk phone closer and picked up the receiver.

***

"Yes, sir," Nate said. "We're diverting now."

Tomlinson's call had broken the tense silence in the SUV, and Nate was glad to have something else to focus on. CHP set up a roadblock near Loma Linda, and Tomlinson wanted him and

Bronsky to oversee the operation and prevent further trouble from the Chinese agents.

The tech team was still tracking down the other two trucks and should be able to pinpoint their locations within the hour. Every NSA agent within a hundred miles was on alert, waiting for the signal to deploy.

They just needed to draw in the net carefully and not let their fish escape.

"Wait in the vehicle," Nate said to Thaddeus and Declan when they pulled in behind the roadblock.

The CHP had set up at the bottom of a small hill so that oncoming traffic wouldn't be alerted to their presence until it was too late to turn around. They waved cars through two openings in the barricade while on alert for the suspect vehicle. Two officers waited with spike strips several hundred yards up the road, should they be needed. Everyone wore body armor and helmets—not taking any chances after the recent loss of two fellow officers.

Nate and Steve approached a tall sergeant in a helmet and leather jacket. He wore old-style, mirrored aviator sunglasses and had a thick, dark mustache. Steve was absent-mindedly whistling "YMCA" until Nate shot him a warning glance.

The two agents showed the officer their credentials and began asking questions while they continued to scan the oncoming traffic.

Declan craned his neck to investigate the front seat. After a moment, he sat back, a deflated look on his face. "They took the bloody keys."

Sterling arched an eyebrow and looked at him but didn't say anything.

***

A portly man in a dark suit sat in the foyer as Richard and Cara entered the home. It took a moment, but Richard finally recognized Randolph Davis, his father's personal attorney.

"Hello, Richard...Cara," he said, extending a hand. "I'm so sorry for your loss."

Richard looked at the outstretched hand dumbly and then met the man's eyes.

"What do you want, Davis?" he said. "Can't this wait?" He gestured toward his sister. "This has been an awfully long day. Can't you give us some time?"

The man slowly pulled his right hand back to his side. Reaching up with his left, he withdrew a pair of envelopes from his suit pocket. He handed one to each of them, and Richard could see their names scrawled across them in his father's neat, crisp handwriting. Feelings of loss, anger, and guilt roiled inside him. He fought to keep his hand steady as he took the envelope from Davis' outstretched hand.

"I'll leave you two for now," Davis said. "But please know I'm here should you need anything."

The man turned and showed himself out.

Richard and Cara looked at each other, then moved to their father's study. Richard pulled a letter opener from a drawer to slit his envelope, then handed it to his sister. He unfolded the page, leaning against his father's large wooden desk.

Richard,

I have instructed Randolph to deliver this letter to you in the event of my unforeseen death. There is also one that should go to your sister.

I know I was never a good father—certainly not the father you deserved. As I watched you grow up, I guess I saw too much of myself in you. After your mother died, I saw too much of her.

I wanted to build a future where you and your sister could have anything you wanted in life. Your mother tried to tell me that what you wanted was my time. Somehow, I was too engrossed in building the business to listen—to really listen.

When she passed, I convinced myself that she had indulged you too much. That you were soft and weak—and yes, even lazy. I wanted you to be tough so that you'd be ready to take over my company one day. That's why I was so hard on you.

I want to say I'd do it differently if I had it to do over again, but a leopard can't change his spots. Your mother was a good woman, and I didn't deserve her—any more than she deserved what happened to her. In the end, I should have done better—been better. As time goes by and I feel our family growing further apart, I cannot find the right words to bridge the chasm between us.

I will say this. I am proud of you. Your decision to move to Salt Lake and complete your degree shows me that I was wrong about you. I was wrong about a lot of things.

Take care of your sister. You are all each other has now, but I think that will be enough.

Dad

Richard crumpled the letter and tossed it into the trash bin by his father's desk. He moved toward the door, then hesitated, turned around, and retrieved it. He smoothed it out and placed it gently on the desk.

Cara had finished her letter as well and was wiping a tear from her eye. Their eyes met, then Richard hugged her tight. He tried to think of the right thing to say.

"Let's go find something to eat," he said finally. "I'm buying."

***

Liu Wei drove on, occasionally searching his rearview mirror for any sign of trouble. Something wasn't right, though he couldn't put his finger on it. Twice in the last hour, he'd felt a strange tightness in his chest, and now the hairs on the back of his neck were standing on end. Agent Chun had never been the nervous type, and this new feeling—whatever it was—had him both confused and irritated.

Xun and Chen had called half an hour ago using an encrypted cell phone. They'd been pulled over and had shot two police officers to escape. Liu Wei cursed and told them to stick with the plan, stay on their route, and put as many miles behind them as they could. He and Lam would meet them at the rendezvous point in Fullerton.

Nuan Lam turned her attention from the window for the first time in miles.

"But we're not going to Fullerton, are we?" She looked at Liu Wei questioningly.

"If the other two teams are compromised, we can't have the Americans getting any information out of them. I gave both teams a separate meet-up location before we split up. Neither knows the truth. If they make them talk, interrogators won't detect any deception on their part."

Lam bit her lip slightly and turned back to the window. She understood their orders and what was at stake. Still, she kept seeing the image of Richard's father lying in his own blood. Susie Yang was a lie—but now she wasn't sure she was Nuan Lam anymore, either.

***

Theo pressed the gold buttons on the control device one by one and closely observed the starfield hologram as it shifted. Abe theorized that only the seven larger buttons were actual commands or triggered specific actions. The smaller buttons did not appear to produce any noticeable results. They might serve as fine-tuning controls used in conjunction with those buttons with symbols, but there was no way to confirm it without the primary device.

One of the larger buttons had a **ЊЌ** symbol. When Theo pressed it, the image blurred, and the pinpoints of light seemed to flow in from the top of the hologram, disappearing below as new lights moved in.

After roughly ten seconds, the lights slowed and stopped. The displayed stars expanded from the center—the change in perspective resembling a camera lens zooming through space. Finally, the hologram stopped and revealed a noticeably red sphere. Five smaller points circled it, tiny silver beads slowly orbiting the star.

"Those are planets," Abe said. "I'd bet my lunch money on it."

Theo pressed another button, this one containing a Ӿ symbol. A thin, blue, thread-like line originated from the outermost planet and trailed toward the bottom of the image. The view zoomed out once again and followed the line as it traced a path back to where the simulated images began. However, the display zoomed in this time to show a single light point surrounded by nine orbiting silver beads. The line tracked until it connected to the third bead from the star.

"Oh, my gosh ..." Abe said.

"Gosh, indeed," said Theo, smiling. He turned to Lisa. "I think we just found the roadmap in the glove box."

***

"Alright," shouted Sergeant DeSalvo. "Everyone ready. This is it!"

The faded red Ford crested the hill and slowed as its driver noticed the activity and roadblock ahead. Officers moved quickly to close off the barricade, eliminating any pathway through.

The truck came to a full stop in the center of the highway a hundred yards or so from the officers crouching along the shoulder with their spike strips. Travers and Bronsky stood behind one of the parked cruisers alongside Ron DeSalvo.

Nate eyed the shotguns, pistols, and even a few M4s trained on the two figures in the truck's cab. *This could get out of control quickly,* he thought.

"Turn off the vehicle and place both hands out the window." DeSalvo's voice boomed through the bull horn. "You have exactly twenty seconds to comply before we open fire on you."

"Sergeant," Nate said, trying to keep his voice calm, "we need to question these men, and we can't do that if they're dead. I don't need to remind you this involves national security, and our orders are from the very top."

DeSalvo turned on the two NSA agents. His face was unreadable behind the mirrored lenses.

"And I don't need to remind you that two of my own are dead thanks to these *men.* I don't care who you work with—or for. Hell, they can fire me tomorrow, but I'm not letting these two put another of my people in danger."

The next several seconds were a blur. There was a loud *POP!* followed immediately by another. Nate saw Steve drop instinctively. He ducked for cover just as he caught the muzzle flash out of the corner of his eye. Several of the officers at the barricade fired their weapons before DeSalvo ordered them to cease firing.

At least six rounds had shattered the windshield, and a dozen more had pierced the radiator. Hot, green liquid spewed from behind the grill of the truck.

The two officers nearest the truck approached each side, weapons drawn. After a few seconds, one of them called out loudly to the others.

"Clear. Suspects down."

Nate grabbed the trailer key from the glove box as the CHP officers secured the scene.

Initially, it appeared that the two suspects had fired at the officers at the roadblock, who had responded by returning fire. Nate's combat experience told him the two men likely shot themselves rather than be captured.

The single padlock key was the only one on the keyring. Nate unlocked the trailer then swung the doors wide in anticipation. Sunlight poured in, illuminating the floor of the empty space. *Damn,* he thought.

Miles away, Liu Wei received the last encoded text from team three. Agents Xun and Chen were dead.

***

Chapter 13

In the aftermath of the freeway fiasco, Nate had pulled rank—in a manner of speaking. He ordered the CHP to stand down but promised Sergeant DeSalvo he would provide any evidence they found relating to the murder of the two motor officers.

He understood the bond this man felt with his men and had experienced the frustration of losing a close team member and friend.

An NSA forensic team arrived and began cataloging the truck, its occupants, and anything else that might help them track down the other Chinese agents. The contents of the truck's cab were spartan, to say the least; there were no bags, wallets, or papers of any kind other than the vehicle registration (which was falsified) and the driver's Nevada license, which was likely a forgery as well.

Nate stepped over to where Steve spoke with one of their fellow agents.

"Well, we'd better get Tomlinson on the horn and see what our next move is," he said.

They climbed into their SUV, and Nate started the engine. The men in the back seat had been so quiet he nearly flinched when the Irishman spoke up.

"Oy, I'm guessin' they didn't have the device, did they?"

"No," Nate said. "There's not much here to go on. I'm going to see where they want us to head next."

He pulled onto the highway and turned west.

His call with Tomlinson confirmed what they already suspected. The other two trucks were headed toward LA, each using a different stretch of highway. Another team was closing in on a white Chevy near Barstow; the tan Chevy had followed a network of state roads, and they'd lost sight of it when it pulled into the San Bernardino Forest near Big Bear Lake.

Steve pulled up a map search on his tablet while Nate continued to talk with their boss.

"My money's on the tan Chevy," Steve said, tracing his finger across the screen. "The other two are decoys. We need to get to Big Bear."

Tomlinson agreed, and Nate continued along I-10. He hoped they still had enough time to intercept the Chinese agents before they got into LA. In a city that large, it would be almost impossible to find them.

"There's another thing," Tomlinson said. "Gerald Hayes didn't make it. He died just after four this morning."

"How's Richard doing?" Sterling asked, trying to be heard from the back seat.

"Ah...Doctor Sterling. I'm sorry. I forgot you were there as well."

"Seems to be a lot o' that goin' around," Declan said almost under his breath.

"Richard and his sister left the hospital around seven. I believe they were going home," Tomlinson said.

Seeing the look of concern on Sterling's face, Declan said, "Richie's tougher than he looks, Professor."

***

Liu Wei had one last trick up his sleeve. As they pulled up the mountain road leading toward Big Bear Lake, he pulled the truck under a makeshift canopy about fifty yards from the road. The thick trees would make aerial surveillance nearly impossible.

Two men waited nearby, and together the four of them pushed the trailer into a waiting delivery truck, securing it in place. As Liu Wei prepared to drive the large delivery truck back the way they had come, the other two men quickly masked the windows of the pickup. They painted the Chevy with green, brown, and black splotches, creating a passable camouflage pattern in a few minutes.

The Chevy continued along the lake road and then turned toward the city of San Bernardino.

"You have been very quiet, Nuan Lam," Liu Wei said. "Are you unsure where your loyalties lie?"

He gave her a probing look that made her uncomfortable. She met his stare with a look of stoic determination. She wasn't going to appear weak in front of this man.

"No, not at all. My loyalties are unchanged. I want nothing more than to complete the mission and go home to my family." She softened a bit and gave him a weary smile. "Agent Chun, the past several days have been more than I am used to. That is all it is. I'm just exhausted."

He looked at her a moment longer, then returned his eyes to the road, apparently satisfied.

Nuan Lam's conflicted thoughts turned back to her country, her family, her duty, and finally—her friends.

***

Bronsky was right—the second truck was also a decoy. NSA operatives took the driver without incident just outside Barstow when he stopped for gas. They'd loaded him into a secure van and transported him to LA for interrogation.

The contents of the truck mirrored those found in the Ford. The trailer was empty. They now knew for sure where the device wasn't. Unfortunately, the third truck had essentially disappeared.

Satellite imagery confirmed it traveled along the state highway headed west toward the lake. As the trees grew thicker, visibility became spotty. The truck turned off onto a side road, and the cameras could no longer see it.

The satellite was not directly overhead, and the angle made it impossible to penetrate the overgrowth. The Chinese agents must have known this and planned accordingly.

Tomlinson rubbed his aching shoulder through the heavy bandage and sling and cursed under his breath. *How are they staying one step ahead of us?* he thought. The fact that they were so coordinated and well organized irritated him more than he wanted to admit.

The Chinese government could not have known about the artifact in advance, which meant they already had several entire teams on American soil ready to mobilize. Tomlinson himself had alluded to this exact possibility when meeting with the NSA deputy director and certain members of congress. However, he didn't really believe the threat was as critical as he made it out to be. In fact, he'd used a well-known boogeyman to persuade them to increase his department's funding and decrease operational oversight.

Yang obviously tipped these agents off when her group realized they had something of value. *They had to have agents in Denver, Las Vegas—certainly Los Angeles,* he thought. *Just how deep does this go?* The telephone on his desk rang, and he was grateful for the interruption.

"Sir? It's Abe. Abe Jensen."

"Yes, Abe. It's only been a few hours. I still remember who you are."

There was no mistaking the edge in his voice, only partially aimed at the young agent.

"Uh...Yes, sir. Sorry ..."

"What is it, son? Why did you call? Spit it out." *Alright, dial it back a little,* he thought. He took a long slow breath and waited.

"We've had a breakthrough here, sir." The excitement in Abe's voice was evident even through the distortion of the phone.

"Doctor Stirling thinks he has the control module figured out. We can't be sure until we can test it with the device."

Now Tomlinson sat up in his chair.

"Listen to me carefully," he said. "Does Stirling think he can activate the device using the module?"

"No, sir. We tried that. Apparently, something is interfering with the signal, or the device must be powered up for the control module to work. But there's another thing." Abe paused as if searching for the right words, then pushed ahead. "Doctor Kowalski says the device powered up on its own after their first two controlled experiments. She was about to call Mr. Hayes, but the effect reversed itself. The agents who stole it struck right after that, and she forgot about it in all the commotion."

Tomlinson hung up without another word and dialed Travers's cell number.

***

Declan stared out the window as the SUV rolled toward Big Bear Lake. He marveled at the tall pines and thick willow and aspen groves. It was a far cry from the hot, dusty desert they had just crossed after leaving Las Vegas—or the desert outside Moab, with its deep red stone and sands.

Dozens of side roads—some paved, some not—branched off from the main highway in several directions. There was no way they could search them all. Houses lined some streets; smaller trails led to cabins further back among the trees.

Travers slowed and pulled to the shoulder to allow a large box truck to pass on their left. The cab was dark, and the trees cut the sunlight significantly, making it impossible to see either the driver or his passenger.

Still, for the briefest of moments, Declan felt that the woman in the passenger seat had been staring at him intently.

Then Travers's phone rang, and the moment passed.

***

Chapter 14

"No, sir. We're just east of the lake, but there are so many cabins and dirt roads in the area; they could be anywhere." Rather than take the call hands-free, Nate had pulled further off the road and taken out his cell. After a brief pause, he placed his hand over the speaker and turned to his two passengers. "He wants to know if the device activated or lit up or did anything else on its own before it...uh...transported you all back to Utah."

"No," Sterling said. "We didn't know what it was or what it did until we hit it with the laser in my son's lab in Denver."

"Hold on, Professor," Declan piped up. "Richie said he felt the magnetic field was gettin' stronger once we got to the university. Theo mentioned it, too."

"Well, yes, but we didn't know it was related to *powering on* or anything at the time."

Nate relayed this back to his boss. After a moment, he leaned across Bronsky's lap, drawing a strange look from his partner. He opened the glove box and rooted around inside.

"No, sir. It doesn't look like we've got a compass in the vehicle," he said.

"Yer holding one," Declan said. "Don't they teach you spy-types anythin'?"

He explained how they could use their phone's magnetometer in the same way as a compass. In fact, they could download a compass app in less than a minute. Nate finished his call with Tomlinson and added the app to his phone. He handed it to Steve as he pulled back onto the highway.

"Hold it by the window," Nate said. "Let me know if the needle changes direction."

Bronsky watched as the displayed needle went from pointing behind them to pointing ahead and to their right.

"That way!" he said, pointing up a nearby dirt road.

No one registered that the needle had been briefly pointing east, back the way they had come, before spinning back to the north. It had also been pointing in the direction the moving truck had gone.

***

They gassed up the truck one last time before they reached their destination. As usual, Lam stayed in the vehicle in case a security camera captured her face. With everything they'd done to avoid detection, they couldn't afford any slipups this close to the finish line.

Liu Wei topped off the tank and went inside to purchase a couple of hot dogs and sodas.

Lam watched him enter the convenience store, then quickly pulled her phone from her purse and scrolled through her contacts. Her father's name flashed by, as did Doctor Stirling's. She finally settled on the one she wanted and quickly typed a string of characters, then hit *SEND* before placing the phone back in her purse. Liu Wei reached his arm through her window unexpectedly, and she had to stifle a scream.

"I hope you're okay with just mustard," he said, handing her a foil-wrapped hot dog and a can of Coke.

Back on the interstate, Liu Wei and Lam headed toward Newport Beach, then pulled onto a large lot with several metal buildings.

The sign on the gate read *Asia Vintage Auto.*

Lam tried to stay out of the way as several men—all MSS agents—hoisted the device and lowered it into a modified red and white 1958 Plymouth Fury. The agents had removed the engine and hastily welded a special copper-clad steel cage to the motor mounts. Liu Wei had told her they needed an older car with an engine compartment large enough for the device.

Now he stood talking with the others, his back turned.

I won't get a better chance than this, she thought, quickly reaching under the hoses and wires affixed to the cover they'd placed over the device.

At first glance, it looked like a standard big block engine with air filters, headers—even a distributor cap. These were only window dressing that the men had attached to a large metal plate. It sat atop the device and was strapped down tight on either side to prevent it from shifting in transit.

"What are you doing, Nuan Lam?"

She hadn't seen Liu Wei approach, and he'd startled her yet again—but she maintained her composure this time. Unfazed, she pointed to one of the straps near where she was standing.

"This strap looked loose. I was just trying to tighten it."

He leaned in for a better look and tugged on the end of the tie-down. It gave a half-inch, and Lam's breath caught in her throat.

"Good catch," he said.

She relaxed when he gave the other straps a fleeting glance, then turned his attention back to the men preparing to load the car into a large metal shipping container. Her heart raced, and she felt a brief wave of nausea. Her pulse made a deep, low hum in her ears.

***

It appeared Tomlinson hadn't used up all of his luck after all. One of Jensen's former coworkers had intercepted a text message sent from Yang's phone. When it went missing along with the student agent, he contacted the Utah Data Center and told them to run a regular scan of the Stingray towers around LA for Yang's unique phone ID.

Like many other states, California used IMSI catchers (Stingrays) for surveillance. They mimic cell towers but trick nearby cell phones into transmitting their locations.

Yang's phone was in LA—West Covina, to be exact. She had sent the text message to Richard Hayes, although the device had fried his cellphone along with Cole's.

Yang would have known that—which was why Tomlinson was dubious about the text and her intentions for sending it. At first glance, it seemed innocuous enough:

Richard, I'm sorry for everything, FWIW. I know you will get through this, IMO - 9213761. I hope you find what makes you happy B4N </3.

Tomlinson felt she was trying to say more without coming right out with it—as if she feared discovery. *But by who?* he thought. *Us? The agents she was traveling with?* He reread the message, trying to read between the lines. He was no expert in text-speak, but having a teenage daughter, he'd learned the basics just to keep up.

He knew FWIW meant "for what it's worth," IMO was "in my opinion," B4N was "bye for now." The other symbols at the end represented a broken heart. It was the string of numbers that didn't seem to fit.

On a whim, he entered the numbers into a search window on his computer. It listed several items whose catalog number matched or contained the string—including a genetic research study on the

NIH website and several other seemingly random entries. He scrolled down the page, seeing nothing of importance—no connection. Then his eyes fixed on one entry:

IMO-9213761 - Vessel DONG TIAN JIN - Container Ship.

***

Liu Wei supervised as the last of the containers were loaded onto the semi-trucks to transport them to the seaport. Then, one by one, the massive trucks trundled out of the lot and onto the highway.

In addition to the Plymouth, several Bel Airs, a '63 Corvette, and a '69 GTO were among the fourteen vintage vehicles distributed throughout the containers destined for China.

The country's growing economy allowed some wealthy business leaders the luxury of collecting classic cars—among other things. As a result, vintage vehicle exports had increased significantly in the past decade to meet this demand.

Liu Wei felt confident his superiors would be pleased with the creative way he had executed his plan.

The *Dong Tian Jin,* docked at LA's China Shipping terminal, was already loading containers into its hold. The ship was scheduled to leave port in less than five hours.

The Americans were chasing ghosts, and the object would be in international waters on its way to Beijing before Liu Wei's NSA counterparts figured out they'd been played.

A pleased smile spread across his face as he reveled in his success.

"What happens now?" Nuan Lam asked.

Despite his initial misgivings about working with the girl, she had proved herself useful and had been instrumental in feeding him the information he needed to obtain the device. Now that the object was secure and his mission was complete, however, she was a liability.

Liu Wei could fade back into the woodwork and await new orders—a new assignment. Unfortunately, Lam was too conspicuous; her face was likely on every watch list from here to Canada. He would need to get rid of her.

***

Theo and Lisa watched in awe as Abe deftly navigated his way through the series of commands, expertly pressing each button in sequence.

"I knew all those years I spent playing video games would pay off someday," Abe said with a devious smile. "I just wish my dad could see me now!"

Theo had pulled up some astrological charts on his tablet and, after a few recalculations, could match up some of the more prominent stars. He had to account for the shift in perspective; all the star charts available only showed the position of stars as seen from Earth.

Finally, Theo was able to identify the binary star system that appeared to be the home base—or starting location—for the device as the Kepler-62 system—nearly a thousand light-years away.

They sat in stunned silence, taking in the sheer magnitude of this revelation.

***

Chapter 15

Somehow, the damned Americans had found out the name of the ship Liu Wei planned to use to smuggle out the device. His contacts at the port cautiously decided to offload the containers further down the dock, near an empty berth. Liu Wei argued it wasn't necessary—they were only making more work for themselves. He'd been so confident he couldn't see how the Americans could stop him.

Now he watched helplessly from his hiding place several hundred feet from the ship as American agents forced the ship's crew to line up on the dock. The entire shipping facility was crawling with people from multiple agencies.

It seems Liu Wei had become the mouse after all.

He hadn't realized what was happening at first. So many agents had arrived so quickly that they had almost cornered him along the dock. Fortunately, he'd had the presence of mind to hide.

He had moved toward the ship before ducking out of sight behind a nearby semi-truck at the last second. Two FBI agents, a man and a woman, had strode within ten feet of him, and he'd gripped his pistol and held his breath waiting while they passed.

He wondered if they somehow tracked him- or worse—if Nuan Lam had tipped them off. *Well, she's gone now,* he thought. He couldn't ask her. Not that it mattered anyway.

He had no more aces up his sleeves. If he wanted to salvage this mission, he would have to develop a new plan quickly. The MSS didn't look kindly on failure.

***

Nate drove like a bat out of hell, trying to close the distance between their current location and the waterfront.

The dirt road near Big Bear Lake had been a bust, and Tomlinson had issued new instructions when they entered the highway. They had just reached the outskirts of West Covina when Tomlinson called with the ship name and berth 103.

FBI, TSA, and NSA agents swarmed the entire port, closing it down tighter than Fort Knox.

Nate and Steve showed their credentials at the security gate leading onto Smith Island, where China Shipping—and the *Dong Tian Jin*—were located. The guard leaned close and questioned them about the two men in the back seat.

"I'll need to see their badges as well," the man said. "This is a secure area."

"They're consultants," Steve said matter-of-factly before anyone could say anything else. "Experts in terrorism involving radioactive materials. The head of Homeland Security—your boss—has reason to believe we may have a potential dirty bomb in one of those." He jerked a thumb toward several mismatched stacks of colored steel shipping containers. "Now, are you gonna let us pass, or do you want to wait until everything from here to downtown glows in the dark?"

The guard looked stricken, and the color drained from his face, leaving a pair of red splotches on his cheeks. He sprinted around the front of the Rhino and frantically waved them through.

When they were out of earshot of the guard shack, Steve muttered under his breath. "We don't have to show you no stinkin' batches!"

Nate burst out laughing. A moment later, the two in the back seat joined him.

***

Think! Liu Wei told himself. He couldn't move far from where he stood with so many eyes sweeping the docks. He tried to look casual, just another dockworker going about his business, oblivious to the swarms of agents everywhere he looked. Liu Wei was glad he'd had the presence of mind to keep the *MAINTENANCE* coveralls he'd used the day before in Denver. As the sun sunk toward the horizon, he found it difficult to believe how much he'd been through in just a short time. Liu Wei was so close to completing his mission and had executed his plan flawlessly up to this point. Now he was a cornered animal—with no idea how he would secure the device and make his escape.

A black SUV stopped between Liu Wei and the ship, and he slipped between two rusted green containers just as four men exited the vehicle. He immediately recognized the two NSA operatives, the other two men he didn't know. They all appeared to be discussing something and focusing their attention on the ship and its crew; they hadn't even looked in his direction. He scanned the nearest shipping unit—the one with the Plymouth inside—to see if there was a way to climb on top. He grasped the upright door latch poles firmly, one in each hand. Then, using the ridges in the steel doors like makeshift rungs, Liu Wei climbed onto the top of the container. He hoped he might be able to lie low while he thought about his possible options.

***

They parked the SUV and exited the vehicle in a clear space between container stacks. The Irishman arched his back, and Steve heard a series of pops that sounded like he'd stepped on a sheet of bubble wrap.

The two had been cooped up back there with minimal breaks for most of the day. It had to be especially rough on the big guy. *Good*, Steve thought as he remembered the question mark in the middle of his face that used to be his nose.

A couple of men in tailored suits—FBI for sure—had the captain and some twenty-odd crew members seated near the base of one of the giant green cranes used to load the ungeared ships. Steve surveyed the stacks of containers still waiting to be loaded. *There must be a few hundred, just in this berth alone. So how the hell are we gonna find the right one?* He pulled his phone from his pocket. "You think the magnet-compass thing will work around all this metal?"

"If the magnetic field is strong enough, it ought to pull the needle away from true north at the very least," said Sterling. "If the two of you split up along either side of each stack, you should be able to see if the field affects your compass."

"Alright. Sterling, you're with me," said Nate. "Steve, you've got Cole."

That's just great, Steve thought.

They walked back and forth between the towering containers stacked like oversized, multicolored building blocks. The compass needles shifted occasionally but never enough to warrant further examination, so they moved on to the next pile.

As Steve rounded the far end of one stack, the on-screen needle suddenly moved a full ninety degrees. It now pointed *away* from them and toward an area where just a dozen or so containers sat side by side, not vertically like the others.

"Are you seeing this?" he asked Cole.

"Yeah," the Irishman said, looking up and shading his eyes. The sun dropped even lower on the horizon. "It's pointing southwest."

***

Liu Wei dropped to a prone position just as the dark-haired agent and the giant man he was with turned from the stacks destined for the deck of the *Dong Tian Jin.* The NSA agent had his cell phone and was obviously tracking the device somehow.

Though he could no longer see them, he heard their shoes scuffing the pavement surface. They were standing feet away, and he couldn't do anything. If they managed to open the unit, they would recover the device. If he allowed that to happen, Liu Wei would be humiliated by his failure. Then, the MSS could reassign him to a nonessential position, ship him back to China...or worse.

***

It wasn't hard to figure out which container held the device. The compass direction hadn't changed as Steve and the Irishman crossed the open space and zeroed in on a dark blue unit. Steve could feel the brute breathing down his neck. *Why the hell is he standing so close, and why does it irritate me so badly?*

Steve felt like he was about to jump out of his skin. It was as if he had ants all over him.

"Look," Steve snapped, "why don't you wait over there until I make sure no surprises are waiting."

He pocketed his phone, drew his pistol, and stepped toward the corner of the steel box rather than approach the doors face-on.

"Suit yerself," the Irishman said with a shrug as he stepped out of sight behind one of the other containers.

Steve kicked at the heavy-duty zip-tie-like closure preventing the latching mechanism from releasing. Taking a deep breath, he pulled the handle to unlatch the doors. He silently counted to three, then threw them wide, dropping into a combat stance.

He didn't see anyone inside the container, but he didn't see the object, either. Staring blankly, he tried to process just *what* he saw. Glossy crimson and white paint and gleaming chrome. A pair of old-fashioned headlights stared back at him from inside the steel box. It was a '58 Plymouth, no question about it. He'd seen this car before, or one like it—the movie had given him nightmares when he was ten.

As Steve stood with his gun drawn down on the antique car, he felt the hairs on his neck standing on end.

Are the headlights actually glowing?

He blinked and tried to swallow his panic. The brightening lights held him in their menacing stare. He both felt and heard an other-worldly vibration that shook his bones. He stood, slack-jawed and rooted to the spot as the car began to rock violently on its wheels, blue light leaking under its hood. The hum grew louder and more intense, and Steve *knew* he was going to die.

Suddenly a strong hand grasped him by the collar and flung him like a ragdoll across the pavement. The physicality of the contact broke his paralysis, and he began running toward Nate and Sterling, with the Irishman close behind him.

"Get down!" Nate shouted, drawing his weapon. A searing pain erupted in Steve's hip, and he toppled to the ground. He looked back in time to see the Asian man drawing down on him just as a blinding white flash obscured his vision.

***

Chapter 16

The taxi pulled up to the LAX passenger drop-off area in front of the Tom Bradley International terminal. The sour-faced driver waited barely long enough for Nuan Lam to step away before speeding off without a word. Liu Wei had paid the driver (not allowing much for a tip, she noticed) when he'd unceremoniously dumped her in the taxicab outside of Lakewood.

Lam was quite relieved to be far away from Liu Wei. His mannerisms and body language suggested he'd begun to suspect her of possibly double-crossing him. In addition, he'd been acting increasingly paranoid and agitated as they were leaving the vintage auto lot.

She knew he wouldn't hesitate to put a bullet in her head if he thought she was jeopardizing *his* mission. Fortunately, Liu Wei hadn't seen her slip her phone into the red car's engine compartment—or that she'd unplugged the electrical connection on the copper-clad dampening cradle in which the device sat.

As she stepped into the building, Lam caught sight of a pair of uniformed officers. She lowered her gaze and feigned searching through her purse as she passed them. When neither turned nor tried to stop her, she let out the breath she wasn't aware she'd been holding.

She glanced around, seeing several more individuals with uniforms. Some were LA county sheriffs; most, though, were US customs agents. Ahead and to her right, she saw a shop with the words *Sunglass Shack* above the door. She quickly crossed and stepped inside.

***

Hector Rodriguez stood against a large pillar, watching passengers queue up at the China Air check-in counter. His supervisor had radioed him to search for a specific passenger, and he was pretty sure he had eyes on her.

Hector had been with Customs and Border Protection for nearly ten years. He'd intercepted numerous drug shipments—both on and in passengers—and even had a hand in thwarting a human trafficking operation.

Most of the time, though, he stood around watching for suspicious behavior or nervous-looking passengers.

He'd never been involved in capturing a spy before.

Apparently, the NSA had put out several urgent watch memos for a person of interest accused of spying for China. They input her likeness into the facial recognition programs used in airports and train and bus terminals all over LA.

The security team got a hit from the cameras in the international terminal. Hector and two other team members had been alerted to intercept her before she could board her flight.

Watching someone without letting them know they are under surveillance was a skill Hector had honed through years of practice—and one he was quite proud of. He nonchalantly scanned the crowd, keeping his face neutral. Hector never made eye contact with the individual they were observing. Instead, he confirmed their location with each sweep of his gaze.

He did, however, make eye contact with Tisha and Jamal.

They confirmed with a look and a nod that they also had eyes on the subject.

The young Asian woman dropped off her luggage and tucked her boarding pass into her purse as she walked toward the TSA security checkpoint. Hector stepped up behind her as the other two moved to block her path.

"What is this?" the woman said. Her eyes moved from Jamal to Tisha, then back.

Hector gently but firmly grabbed the woman's arm.

"We just have some questions to ask, ma'am," he said. "Would you please come with us?"

"But I haven't done anything," the woman said, trying to pull away. Her voice grew louder and more frantic. "I'm going to miss my flight! You have no reason to hold me!"

Others in the terminal began to notice as the woman grew more belligerent. Hector continued talking in calm, low tones—both to try to soothe the woman and reduce the disruption to other nearby passengers.

Tisha quickly moved to the woman's other side, and Jamal opened a secured door with a key code. They ushered the still protesting woman through, and the door shut tight behind them.

Standing at the New Zealand counter directly across from China Air, Nuan Lam watched the whole scene transpire from behind a pair of oversized frames. She casually brushed away a few strands of silver hair from her stylish wig, then turned her attention back to the pretty blonde behind the counter.

"Love your hair," the young woman said. Her thick Kiwi accent had a pleasant lilt to it.

"Thanks."

Lam slid her new passport—with a new name and matching photo—to the woman. She gave it no more than a cursory glance before handing it back, along with Lam's boarding pass.

"Here you go, Ms. Chang. Terminal B, gate 208," she said, smiling and pointing down the concourse. "Have a nice flight."

***

Theo sat at one of the lab workstations, fiddling with an old battery-operated radio they had found. He spun the dials and finally settled on a classic rock station—anything to fill the too-quiet building.

His stomach growled. He couldn't remember when he'd eaten last, other than some vending machine chips hours ago.

Dr. Kowalski and Abe had driven to Pahrump (a good deal closer than Las Vegas) to pick up pizza for the few lab workers remaining in the facility. He wished they'd hurry back.

The sun was setting quickly, and it would be dark soon. Other than a few technicians working quietly at the far side of the building, the place was a tomb.

Gerald Hayes's death had obviously been brutal on the close-knit group. Considering this, Lisa had told them all to go home.

Most had left, although one team argued that Hayes would want them to finish their work. She couldn't dissuade them from this and accepted that they were all entitled to grieve in the way they saw fit.

Theo suggested maybe she should take her own advice, but she had quickly changed the subject to food.

Something in his peripheral vision attracted his attention, and he turned to investigate. He stared at the ring of blue light on the control device, which had begun cycling brighter than it had since they'd activated it. He looked around the nearby tables and carts, unsure what was happening or what he should do. The lights settled into a pattern of sorts—two quick pulses, then a long, slower pulse. Then the pattern repeated.

Finally, Theo saw a bright, bluish glow coming from the front of the lab, near the damaged door.

Great, he thought. *They're back with the pizza.*

However, as he stood and turned to look in that direction, he could see that the glow was *inside* the building. A large, swirling ball of light hung not more than ten feet from him. Electricity crackled, and he could smell the burning ozone in the air. The pale azure light gained intensity and seemed to breathe with the same rhythm as the lights on the control device. He briefly thought he could see a massive ship through the swirling mass, like a mirage.

The radio let out an ear-splitting, high-pitched wail that threatened to pierce Theo's skull, then fell silent. He shielded his eyes with his arm just as a thunderclap sounded in his ears, and a blinding flash washed away reality.

As his eyes slowly adjusted to the impenetrable darkness, he inched closer to the event's epicenter, feeling his way with trembling fingers. His heart was a jackhammer in his chest.

From somewhere behind the building, he heard emergency generators switch on. The lab was now awash in artificial light again, and Theo found himself staring at a vintage car, probably from the 50s. He willed himself forward, unsure what to make of the implausible sight. His focus on the vehicle was so profound he nearly tripped over the dead man's torso at his feet.

"Theo?" a voice called from his right. "Oh, my God!"

Doctor Kowalski faltered, dropped the pizza boxes, and screamed.

***

Chapter 17

Arthur Tomlinson sat at his desk reviewing the official after-action report he'd submitted not long after they'd recovered the alien teleportation device. For the sake of security, he'd listed it as an *unknown historical artifact.*

To say the deputy director had been displeased about the unwelcome notoriety his little operation had brought to the NSA was an understatement. He'd given Tomlinson an earful on the day he filed his report.

The Chinese agent, identified as Chun Liu Wei, had taken a bullet to his abdomen, causing him to miss Bronsky with his second shot. The wound itself probably wasn't fatal, but now, there was no way to know that. He crumpled to Earth just at the device's magnetic field's perimeter (or, as Sterling called it, event horizon). The forces involved violently tore him in two.

Given the trail of havoc and devastation the man left in his wake, Tomlinson wasn't too choked up about Chun's death.

Bronsky's shooting left him with a fractured pelvis, and he would be off his feet for a while.

At least I won't have to look at his face again until it heals, Tomlinson thought as a wry smile crossed his lips.

Nate's quick thinking and cool marksmanship under pressure probably saved his partner's life. The deputy director was going to recommend both men for citations. Tomlinson shuddered to think how close they had come to losing the alien device to the Chinese government.

NSA data miners had also uncovered the identity of Yang Shu. Too late, they determined Nuan Lam had boarded a flight to Auckland, then traveled on to Guangzhou. However, Chun would likely have succeeded if not for her change of heart—and the auspiciously timed text message. When they extracted the device from the Plymouth, they found she had wedged her phone in alongside it.

Tomlinson's new cell phone rang, and he was surprised to see the call was from Richard Hayes.

"Mr. Tomlinson, the prototype is coming along faster than anticipated. I think we'll have a working model to show to the top brass in, say, a couple of weeks."

"That's good to hear, Mr. Hayes." He paused, waiting for the *but.* In his years of dealing with politicians, the military, and government contractors, these conversations *always* had a *but.*

"But...the reason I called was to ask you a favor," Hayes continued.

Always a 'but,' Tomlinson thought.

***

The tests the previous day had been flawless. Richard was beaming as he met Dr. Kowalski in the immense hangar at the Groom Lake site.

He never dreamed he'd end up at Area 51 about to test the most advanced piece of technology ever seen on earth. *Well, in the past hundred million years, anyway*, he thought.

The SPARC team's endeavors in constructing the Tele-Skipper (he still wasn't sure about the name) in such a short span were exemplary.

It was functional, but they had also put a great deal of effort into the aesthetics. It looked sleek and aerodynamic, though not designed to move in the traditional sense.

Richard had Lisa's marketing sense to thank for that. She had worked tirelessly to meet their commitment over the past few weeks, proving that his father's trust in her abilities had been well-founded.

The Tele-Skipper sat on delicate, graceful runners, like those of a helicopter or sled. They were splayed out wider than necessary to provide excellent stability on any terrain. The two-seat cockpit was airtight, yet it felt more like a car than a spacecraft when sitting at the control panel. The curved windscreen provided excellent visibility.

The teleportation module was nestled into a custom-fitted cage in the center of the craft, with electrical feeds positioned over the depression in each facet.

In the aft section sat the reason the US government had awarded SPARC the contract to build the Tele-Skipper—a proprietary battery designed to convert light to power, then back to light.

All the invited dignitaries were studying the device, asking questions, and striking up conversations with members of Richard's team—or each other. Richard nodded to the two men from the NSA, Tomlinson and Travers.

A five-star general from the Joint Chiefs of Staff introduced himself as Bill Hancomb.

He'd fought in Vietnam, Granada, and the first Gulf War—and had the chest candy to prove it. However, now he bore the plump, well-fed look politicians and other leaders get when they spend more time attending fancy dinner parties than doing any physical work.

Richard wondered if this man had assaulted as much as a flight of stairs in years.

"General Hancomb," Richard said, "allow me to introduce my head of operations, Lisa Kowalski."

Lisa shook the man's hand politely, then excused herself to prepare for the demonstration. The general looked her up and down as she walked away, and Richard suppressed the urge to call him out on it.

"This little flightless bird of yours will be a gamechanger," Hancomb said, turning his attention back toward Richard.

"Yessir. The Russians and the Chinese will have no choice now but to be on their best behavior."

Richard stood thinking for a long moment after that. Then he passed through several other generals and their aides and both senators from Nevada, shaking hands and making polite conversation as he worked his way toward the seating platform set at the back of the massive space.

All the while, the general's words echoed in his brain.

Declan, Theo, and Doctor Sterling sat off to one side of the platform. The two younger men looked miserably out of place in suits and ties.

"Thanks for coming," Richard said. "I had to pull some strings, but I wanted you to be here for this. You were all there at the very beginning, and I think it only fair you get to see what happens next." He turned to Theo. "How'd you like to give us a hand with the demonstration?"

***

"If I can have your attention," Richard said, "we're about to begin. Please take your seats. Everyone should have a pair of protective lenses attached to your chair."

He had to raise his voice to be heard above the din of multiple conversations. As everyone shuffled to a folding chair and donned the tinted safety glasses, he continued.

"As many of you know, my colleagues and I were the first humans to be teleported by this device less than a month ago. The experience was disorienting, to say the least, and somewhat terrifying, if I'm being honest. Though, speaking as a Nevada boy, that might just be because we ended up in Utah."

He paused for the small trickle of laughter.

"We had no idea what it was, where it came from, who built it—nothing. We activated it purely by accident, and it's a wonder we all survived. With the generous resources provided by the US government and the innovative expertise at SPARC, I'm here today to demonstrate that the Tele-Skipper design is one hundred percent safe."

A man in a lab coat stepped forward, carrying a wire cage with a chicken in it. The chicken wore a comical fitted astronaut suit. Richard pulled the chicken from its enclosure and held it up for the others to see.

"I give you, Cluck Rogers!"

This comment elicited a hearty laugh from the visitors. Richard moved to the Tele-Skipper and attached a specially designed clip to the back of the chicken's suit, preventing it from reaching the controls or moving about the cockpit.

The batwing door closed and sealed with a *hiss*.

As he stepped away from the Tele-Skipper, Richard nodded to one of his technicians.

After deciphering the functions of the control module, Abe and Theo had continued to work on the project—although Richard had to convince the NSA and UC Denver to free up their schedules.

The two had come up with a clever method for remote operation so that it didn't require a human onboard to operate the device while they tested it for safety.

One curious thing they found was that the device would not operate without a living creature within the magnetic field. Theo suggested it might be a failsafe to prevent a traveler from being stranded light-years from home.

They had tried house plants at first but without success. Next, they used mice. Unfortunately, these were likely too small to register and deactivate the failsafe. They had discussed using a monkey, but Dr. Kowalski was opposed to any primate research. Enter Cluck Rogers.

"If I could direct your attention to the video screen," Richard said, still backing away. "As you can see, we have several cameras set up in a hangar like this one in size and shape at the other end of this base. But we could send the device just about anywhere. The technology is really quite remarkable."

The technician powered up the device, and everyone could feel the building static on their hair and skin. The now-familiar low hum began, and the air around the Tele-Skipper took on an azure glow.

The shielding cage focused the teleport module's energy, preventing the type of surge that had taken out the power in Theo's lab and later at SPARC.

Now the throng of onlookers witnessed a similar field in the other hangar displayed on the large monitors.

With a brilliant burst, the Tele-Skipper disappeared.

On the oversized screens, they could see where the craft now sat on a small platform set up just for this demonstration. Everyone watched as a female technician raised the door, unclipped Cluck Rogers, and held him up to the camera.

The crowd's initial incredulity melted to raucous applause.

"Okay, Theresa," Richard said into a small microphone. "Have them send it back, please. I think a few folks here would like a photo op."

The process they had all watched moments ago repeated itself on the overhead displays.

Same blue light, same deep hum.

The only thing missing this time was the sensation from the static field. The group watched in patient silence as the swirling blue field engulfed the Tele-Skipper—and it winked out of existence.

They were silent at first. Then some of the visitors closest to Richard saw the look of pure panic on his face, and one by one, they began to realize what they had just witnessed.

"Theresa, what happened?" Richard tried—somewhat unsuccessfully—to keep his voice even and professional.

"Where is the Tele-Skipper?" his voice was shaking, and he was turning a shade of green.

There was a long pause. Those watching this exchange could see the young technician was talking with someone off-screen. Finally, she returned to the camera—her face contrite.

"Sir, the remote unit on this end must have malfunctioned. First, the technician could not get it to respond to his commands. Then the unit cycled into a surging power spike, and he couldn't reverse the phase-out."

"If he wasn't controlling it, HOW DID THE DAMN DEVICE POWER ON?!" His voice became a screech now, and spittle flew from his lips as he spoke. Doctor Kowalski moved in quickly, trying to calm him down. She ushered him through a side door and into a waiting car.

At the same time, Theo entered from the opposite end of the building.

"What did I miss?" he said, rejoining his father and Declan.

"I'm not sure," Thaddeus said, staring at Theo for a long time. He had that look on his face again.

***

"I swear, Richard, you should get an Oscar for that performance," Lisa laughed. "For a minute, I actually thought you *were* losing it."

"Well, I had to sell it," Richard said. "With the NSA and Joint Chiefs there breathing down my neck, anything less would have aroused suspicion."

They sat squeezed into the familiar booth at the back of the restaurant. Buck Owens crooned "Act Naturally" from the jukebox as the waitress in her low-cut blouse and Daisy Dukes brought another pitcher of beer.

"I still don't understand," Thaddeus said. "What exactly happened?"

"One of those fat-assed generals said something that got under my skin," Richard said. "They were all so worried that the Chinese would get away with the device they were willing to do almost anything to prevent that. But once we had it secured, they started talking about using it as a threat to keep the Chinese and the Russians in line. I mean, where does it end? We're not mature enough as a species to have this kind of power. It could only lead to conflict."

"So that's when he pulled me aside at the demonstration," Theo said. "Since Abe and I were the ones who figured out the controls for the damn thing, I knew how to operate it. There was a backup module in one of the SPARC vans outside. I just waited for the signal and fired it up. I activated the Tele-Skipper and essentially hit the RETURN TO SENDER button."

They drank a few more moments in silence. The jukebox played Johnny Cash's "A Boy Named Sue."

"You've been awfully quiet tonight, Declan," Richard said.

Declan looked to each of them in turn, finally resting his gaze on Richard.

"I've just been thinkin' is all," he said. "Assumin' yer flying car thing made it back—and assumin' there's anyone there to see it after a hundred million years..."

He lifted his glass and drained it, wiping his mustache on the back of his hand.

"...What I'm wonderin' is this, Richie Boy. What d'ya think they'll make of the chicken?"

***

"The past, like the future, is indefinite and exists only as a spectrum of possibilities." —Stephen Hawking

ABOUT THE AUTHOR

Dave Bench has spent most of his adult life working in the healthcare industry. He developed a renewed interest in writing in 2015 after illustrating ***The New Kid,*** a children's book written by his wife, Liesl, in 1996.

Yes, he can be a bit of a procrastinator.

He has since written and illustrated ***Take Me to The Zoo!*** and ***Take Me to the Beach!*** published under Bench Press Publishing through Lulu.

Dave enjoys writing short stories—primarily speculative fiction. His forthcoming Sci-Fi epic, **An Elegy for Fools** (begun in the summer of 2020), is due to be finished whenever he gets back around to it. He's also had his poetry published.

When he's not writing, Dave enjoys cooking, playing guitar and Hofner electric bass, and spending time with his family (which includes an African Gray parrot with an attitude). Dave lives in the foothills of the Wasatch Mountains in Salt Lake City, Utah.

You can find more at: www.benchpress-publishing.com.

www.ingramcontent.com/pod-product-compliance
Ingram Content Group UK Ltd.
Pitfield, Milton Keynes, MK11 3LW, UK
UKHW040027200726
13854UKWH00001B/404

9 781304 126948